Demetrio has found the good life, putting his devastating past behind him and investing his hard-earned money into a gay bar on the island of Ibiza, or as the locals insist on calling it, Eivissa. With celebrities and other stunning beautiful men roaming the hot-spot island, Demetrio thinks he's found a slice of heaven. When a strange man's small boat capsizes in the Mediterranean, once he's rescued, he seems to be attracted to Demetrio.

The man, however, has amnesia. He has no memory of his name, his life and has no ID. His boat is registered to a Philip Gordon, but the handsome stranger says he doesn't think it's his name. After picking the name Océano, the Spanish word for the sea, he and Demetrio begin an impassioned affair that soon turns disastrous. Océano may not be amnesiac. He may not be the good guy he seems to be and . . . he may not even be gay.

This book was previously published.

Eivissa
Copyright © 2020 A.J. Llewellyn
ISBN: 978-1-4874-2943-0
Cover art by Angela Waters

Published by eXtasy Books Inc or
Devine Destinies, an imprint of eXtasy Books Inc

Look for us online at:
www.eXtasybooks.com or www.devinedestinies.com

Eivissa

By

A.J. Llewellyn

DEDICATION

To my lovely and wonderful Lisa Cunningham whose new friend-ship has been made possible thanks to the internet and the power of the written word. Thank you for being my friend!

I would also like to dedicate Eivissa to the memory of my cousin John whose disappearance inspired this story. Though we found his body a year after he vanished, exactly as described in this tale, we still have many unanswered questions. To all the families of lost men in the world, no greater pain is known than the unknown. My heart goes out to all of you.

CHAPTER ONE

Demetrio leaned back in his chair, casting his gaze over the impossibly blue waters of the Mediterranean Sea. Even the foam was whiter and brighter here. He craned his neck to scan the horizon. Nothing but birds, boats, and beautiful people as far as the eye could see. He still couldn't believe this small strip of paradise was his. Clear as glass, the sea screamed health and vitality. Even now he could see a yachting family in the distance, the women bobbing in the water, their bright bathing caps looking like gigantic flower heads cast into the waves.

He stretched, tilting his head up, his gaze fixed now on the sky. Blue and more blue. He felt his neck muscles loosening. Ah . . . better. A couple of bones snapped back into place as he shook out his shoulders and rolled his neck. 10:00 a.m. and his day was actually just ending . . . or should have been.

But who could sleep with paradise so near?

Now was the time he'd usually be in bed, but since moving from London to Ibiza, or as all the locals and knowledgeable travelers called it, Eivissa, six months ago, he found that he got by very well on catnaps. An hour here, two hours there, and he was good to go.

Demetrio enjoyed a leisurely, delicious breakfast of *pan de horno*, the local island bread, and a couple of hard-boiled eggs at his favorite table. For a moment he felt a small twinge of regret that he'd sent his date from earlier in the morning back to his hotel room. Silly goose was probably still sleeping off the *chupito* shots.

1

He bit into a small warm, buttery loaf from the café Espardel. He could detect the scent of olive oil in the bread, and he put his nose to the loaf in his hand. Ah, bliss. He enjoyed the quiet luxury of having his nightclub terrace empty and all to himself after a long and busy night. It had been a bit jarring crossing over from the off-season winter months to full-scale service once April rolled around, but now he found he liked the madness. Demetrio didn't care that he had an early license and had to close by 3:00 a.m. each day. The gay couple with the building in the old Eivissa town square opposite him had a late-closing license, and they were welcome to it.

Their license, however, expired at seven o'clock in the morning, and the law of the island was that clubs were forced to close from seven until four thirty in the afternoon. This left a lot of club goers feeling aimless, but a lot of beach places had opened up with beds and sofas and did well in the summer months with day-long breakfast menus.

"¡*Hola*, Demetrio!"

"¡Hola!" he called out to the Sugar guys who sauntered past his terrace with cheery waves. Man, they were sexy. Demetrio was intrigued by the gay porn star, Juan-Juan—whose real name was Chenche—and his husband, Stefan, owners of Sugar, the hottest gay bar on the island. They had a 6:00 a.m. license and there were still people lingering on Sugar's main terrace. That's how Eivissa rolled. The quaint Spanish island, with its ancient, crumbling walls and dedicated pockets of fishing villages, had a hard-partying heart.

The old town center had become the gay capital, and rumor had it Chenche and Stefan had called in numerous favors for their coveted license.

It didn't bother Demetrio. In fact, he was surprised how much he *didn't* care. As a real estate property developer back home, he'd been a very competitive guy working himself into an early grave. Diagnosed with a multitude of anxiety and stress-related illnesses, he'd heeded his physician's advice and taken a year off work. It was astonishing that at the age of thirty-five he could need rest . . . Not that he was getting it.

He was working harder than ever in some respects, but for the first time in his adult life, Demetrio felt real pride and satisfaction in his work. He felt sincere joy in each and every day he spent on the island. He loved the surprises each night brought as he opened up and served his customers at Club Dino. He was already getting rave reviews on internet travel sites from the staid Frommer's slightly more hip TripAdvisor, and Trippy websites. All the online travel magazine sites had sent freelance writers to the island, and his club had its own iPad app. He'd been pleased that in a couple of short weeks his club was getting such positive attention. Even foodies rated him highly on Yelp and local Spanish blogs.

And he was even beginning to have a life. On the rare occasions he had a date, they'd slip over to Sugar, where Demetrio enjoyed the luxury of somebody else mixing him a high-voltage cocktail. Partying was fun but not expensive on Eivissa. The restaurants were also sublime. Packed into small spaces, they each produced an astonishing array of mouth-watering and decadent meals. Nothing, however, compared with Chenche's hand-mixed drinks. He and his fellow waiter boys were always gorgeous, and like the owner of Sugar himself, half-dressed.

Demetrio returned his attention to his iPad and the article he'd been reading on the evolution of underwear. Underwear was considered way too much clothing on Eivissa. Demetrio approved of loincloths and minuscule cock-hugging under-pants. He studied the medieval images of codpieces on his screen. They were quite alluring, too.

He cringed as he studied images of long johns. Since he'd left London, the harsh weather, frozen pipes, chilblains, and thermal wear had become a distant, horrific memory.

Sipping his coffee, he found himself smiling. He'd just spent the last three hours dancing with a hot, handsome traveler. They were all just incredibly sexy on Eivissa. Demetrio and his pals liked to joke that ugly people were turned away at customs.

Demetrio savored the gritty sediment on his tongue. He loved every drop of coffee, even the dregs. Why did everything taste better on this island? His gaze drifted over to the venerable Can Alfredo, one of the oldest restaurants on the island. It had changed hands twice since it opened in 1932. Many places were like that. Despite the jolly party atmosphere, there was a staunch tradition of service and customer pleasure here. Mind you, this was typical of Spain in general.

Eivissa, which had its high season in June and quietly went to sleep each October, had been a real eye-opener for Demetrio. April had become the new month for visitors who preferred their partying with fewer people around. One could savor the splendid orchards that were a big part of the island, and the heady scent of lemons strong on the breeze. By June it was too crowded and hot to linger in some of the best scenic spots.

After visiting each summer for the last few years, Demetrio hankered to move here. He'd found his club via an online ad on craigslist and bought it after taking a comprehensive virtual tour. He'd moved here, shocking his friends and family, and spent months renovating the place. He'd been open exactly two weeks and was already seeing the beginnings of a swift return on his massive financial investment.

He turned his head to the statue of San Antoni, the patron saint of the islands, which his stonemason insisted should have pride of place somewhere in the building. "The saint enjoys a good glass of wine," Emile had insisted. Demetrio hadn't noticed this, though he dutifully left a shot glass of the red stuff each week. He enjoyed adhering to the local customs, though it hadn't been easy finding the perfect place for the patron saint of restaurants and bars. San Antoni couldn't face walls or glass, according to local legend. Once Demetrio discovered every commercial venue featured the local saint, he sought to find the appropriate location for *his* statue. His San Antoni stood behind the outdoor wet bar, gazing out to sea, just like Demetrio.

He watched Chenche and his crowd of friends jump into the ocean. He thought about joining them. Truth be told he kind of had a crush on Chenche, who had an open—*very* open—marriage to Stefan. They had been together ten years before marrying in Madrid the previous summer. Demetrio had met them on one of his trips to Eivissa, and they'd encouraged him to move here.

Demetrio knew that when Chenche made trips to the US to shoot porn during the island's off-season, he also booked himself out as a rent boy. He attended each client accompanied by Stefan. Demetrio knew all this because he read the online gay blogs . . . and because, like on any small island, there was gossip.

Chenche didn't rent himself out on Eivissa. Demetrio didn't quite understand since a lot of gay travelers knew who he was and looked him up, but there was a line and he'd drawn it. Eivissa was home. That didn't mean he didn't fool around. He did. But his porn-star career was a big open secret.

As hot as he was, Demetrio couldn't have handled a guy like Chenche as a long-term mate. He wondered how Stefan did it . . . then realized Stefan was so enamored he'd probably put up with anything just to keep the guy close.

They were a great couple, and in spite of their high-flying sex life, they were good businessmen, terrific friends, and great hosts. Their bar was superhot for a reason.

"Demetrio!" Chenche called out to him.

He laughed, waving back.

"Come and swim with us!" Chenche beckoned, not taking no for an answer.

A swim would be nice, now that he thought of it. He held up a finger, shut down his iPad, deposited it inside the club on the bar, and closed up everything. He'd resisted his date's efforts to stay and have some fun in the sack, namely because the guy had been wasted. Now Demetrio was happy he'd exercised good moral judgment. He wandered down Carrer Santa Lucia in his shorts and flip-flops, sunglasses pushed high on his nose.

The beauty of his new home never failed to astonish him. The once-walled city, built by the North African Carthaginian Empire in the seventh century, was topped on its highest peak by a cathedral and the still-walled city square. Both were equally impressive and were Eivissa's calling cards.

Once the Romans had taken over the eastern portion of the Mediterranean, a new empire was ushered in, and Eivissa embodied the unhurried, uninhibited passion one associated with a tropical island. In recent years gay travelers had begun to flock here, and gay men and women moved to the island to find themselves. Here they found freedom, acceptance . . . even love.

Demetrio had found the first two things and secretly hungered for the third.

Perspiration dotted his forehead and the back of his neck by the time he reached the tiny curve of the bay that denoted the gay stretch of Eivissa's white sands of St. Eulalia Beach.

Thanks to Sugar, Demetrio's bar attracted a good, steady stream of spillover clients who liked trying new places and enjoyed the more relaxed atmosphere of Dino's. Demetrio had kept the name when he bought the club and tried to keep its crumbling Spanish interior, but he and Emile had been forced to do a lot of work to keep it looking that way. His patrons loved his cheese and wine nights, and he adored their appreciation. He really did owe Chenche and Stefan a great deal. They were friendly, supportive, and encouraging. They'd even given him Emile's number and that of a fantastic electrician who'd helped rewire his building.

He shucked off his shorts, leaving only his bright-yellow Speedo on. He caught Chenche's predatory grin as he jumped into the sea. Chenche reached out to him as Demetrio hit the frigid water, planting a big wet kiss on his lips beneath the rolling waves. Demetrio hoped his cock didn't reveal the huge attraction he felt for Chenche. He was cold, but his dick was still on red alert. That's how hot Chenche was. It also, not for the first time, struck him as very telling that the man's name, Chenche, meant 'conquer.' How apt.

Demetrio noticed on a regular basis that Chenche sought to seduce every man he met, and damn it, the gay-porn icon was an astonishing kisser. He liked kissing Demetrio a lot for some reason and put a lot of passion into it. His mouth roamed Demetrio's face as Demetrio fought to keep Chenche's hand out of his tiny Speedo below the water's surface.

Demetrio struggled to raise his head and get some air. As he did so, Chenche's mouth moved to his ear.

"One day," he whispered in Demetrio's ear, "one day you will *beg* me to fuck you."

Chenche curled his hand around Demetrio's huge cock under the water. He hardened even more, to the bursting point. Damn. In Demetrio's mind, he begged Chenche to fuck him morning, noon, and night. He'd never met anyone as good-looking as Chenche, or as hung. The guy was very slim, a twinky kind of guy, in fact, with a massive ten-inch weapon between his thighs. He made no bones about wanting Demetrio. Even Stefan had tried to persuade him to play with Chenche.

"I wouldn't be jealous of you," Stefan had said more than

once. "And I would know where he was."

Demetrio felt sorry for Stefan. He wanted to chastise him for pimping for his lover and for putting up with his slutty ways, but hell's bells, here Demetrio was, having the time of his life making out with the son of a gun in the ocean.

Chenche might have been thin, but he was all lean muscle. He dragged Demetrio to the water's edge, lying on top of him on the sand, kissing him.

God help me, I think I'm gonna come. It was like the gay version of *From Here to Eternity*, and each time the cold waves lapped at his body, he felt a fresh tug of sexual tension as Chenche writhed on top of him, grinding their cocks together.

Demetrio tried not to think about how sexy Chenche was. The guy was taken. A whore. Man . . . nothing worked. He wished now that he hadn't bought the deluxe package of twelve of Chenche's movies *and* his life-size dildo from Chenche's website. All he could think of now was the mingled pleasure and pain he'd derive from getting fucked by the hottest whore this side of the whole planet.

Chenche's tongue plumbed his mouth. If the guy had wanted to fuck him right there and then, Demetrio probably couldn't have and wouldn't have stopped him. The others were laughing.

"Now, that's my idea of a wake-up call," one of the other guys said.

Chenche turned off the porno power instantly. He rolled off Demetrio, sitting next to him on the hard, wet sand. He had a hard-on, too, Demetrio was pleased to see. Chenche always confused Demetrio with his way-out greetings. He sat, feeling dazed and horny as all fucking hell. He tugged at his Speedo, sitting up now, feeling foolish.

He watched Chenche kissing one of the other guys before plunging into the water in his tiny swimsuit, paddling over to Stefan, who happily took his wayward man into his arms and kissed him.

Allowing the water to wash over him, Demetrio scooted back into the sea, happier now that his raging erection was hidden from view. He smiled at Stefan, who came over to bob beside him as the others frolicked, splashing each other with eager, childlike glee.

"Did you get any sleep?" Stefan asked.

Demetrio knew Stefan was a born worrier. He was the daddy of the bunch. People dismissed him as a Muscle Mary because he was a big guy with a ton of muscles, and he was so quiet they assumed he was dumb. He was far from it. An attorney by trade, he still practiced law in the off-season. Real estate law was his passion, and thanks to Stefan, Chenche's porn star earnings had been poured into real estate investments throughout Spain. They owned commercial and residential properties and lived well off their investments.

Stephan had figured out how to make a living off cell phone applications like VMS. It was all foreign to Demetrio, but as far as he understood, every time Stefan's cell phone rang with a certain ring tone, indicating it had been delivered via VMS, he made money. People asked him questions, and they paid by phone. It seemed easy, and yet when Stefan tried to explain how it worked, Demetrio quickly lost interest in trying to understand the financial aspects.

Stefan was also the go-to guy for all the club owners on the island, mostly British, who spent the winter months here planning and negotiating big-name musical acts for the summer months. Stephan and Chenche lived on the island year-round, except their brief forays to New York for Chenche's porn shoots. In June, the hottest month on the island in more ways than one, Eivissa would launch its annual music festival. Every club DJ in Europe would make an appearance, and the hottest musical acts would come and do their thing. Thanks to Stefan, Demetrio had a few DJs booked, including the wildly popular Fatboy Slim.

"That was a hot guy you got yourself last night," Stefan said. German born of Spanish parents, he had been educated in public schools all over England. Expelled from many, he'd wound up well educated in spite of himself. His English was impeccable, unlike Chenche's, who, although beguiling, spoke heavily accented and sometimes halting English, but perfect Spanish, French, and Italian. Demetrio adored them both and sometimes wondered why he kept resisting their suggestions of a threesome, but like his father always said, "You don't pee on your own doorstep."

He hated the idea of the threesome causing problems between them. He knew Chenche and Stefan were staunch islanders who remained here even during the off-season. They took their trips to the US for Chenche's movies, but otherwise they stayed right here with a handful of regulars. He hated the idea of anything spoiling their friendship, especially in the long winter months with so few people on the island.

Demetrio was already looking forward to November rolling around. Winter on the island was still great, weather-wise, but the locals slowed down, ate leisurely meals, and really soaked in the atmosphere of island life. Demetrio had been surprised how well he himself had adapted to it.

"Yeah, he was hot." Demetrio wanted to change the subject. The guy, whose name he'd already forgotten, was not only a tourist but, Demetrio had learned, a married British schoolteacher who had come to Eivissa with his male buddies after watching their football team playing through other European countries. He had a yen to experiment with gay sex. Not with Demetrio he wouldn't. The one time he'd been some guy's experiment, it had ended badly. He leaned back, enjoying the warm sun on his face as the water lapped over his thighs.

"You didn't get lucky?" Stefan pressed for details.

"I decided not to . . . . He's not really gay."

Stefan's head snapped in his direction. Demetrio could tell he was thinking about saying something. Stefan was not a garrulous guy. His lover was the life of any party, but when Stefan spoke, he *said* something.

"You know, Chenche was married and straight when I met him."

"Really?"

Demetrio hadn't known that. He glanced at Stefan, who was staring across the horizon as Chenche played in the surf with three hot, hung guys. They were all naked and . . . happy.

"*Sí.* He was married. They had a threesome . . . he said he'd never really enjoyed sex until he sucked his first cock and had a man suck his ass."

Demetrio grinned. "Were you that man?"

A beat, then Stefan nodded. "I was attracted to him. His wife picked me. She wanted to see us together. I don't think she had any idea of what would happen. Our chemistry was . . ." Stefan's fists collided, his hands shooting in the air, miming an explosion. "After that he craved cock, and I . . . I gave it to him." He smiled. "He felt guilty about leaving his wife. They never had children, thank God. They are still friends. He still sends her money when she needs it. She lives in Barcelona."

Demetrio waited, but Stefan said nothing more. He had no idea how long the guy had waited for Chenche, but for Demetrio, moving to Eivissa and meeting hot, sexy gay guys had been appealing. He could have his pick of men, and if one didn't work out, well, there'd be other guys flying in every day. He had no intention of waiting for some guy to figure out his sexuality. He'd done that before, with disastrous results.

"I'm just saying, love comes in unexpected ways," Stefan

said, surprising him.

Demetrio nodded. He knew this was true but hearing this particular piece of philosophy from Stefan stunned him.

"You never know," Stefan said. "Maybe this guy is the one."

Demtrio laughed. "I don't think so. He's married." He thought about the implication of those words and finally got it. Chenche had been married. Now he and Stefan had a life together.

"Time to go," Stefan said, checking his U-Boat watch. "The price of summer, eh? No rest for us."

He stood, reaching a hand down to Demetrio and helping him to his feet.

"You miss winter on the island?" Stefan suddenly asked.

"Very much."

"You'll miss it more and more. It's our prize for dealing with the summer."

The guys threw their shorts back on and they all walked up the hill. Chenche threw a careless arm around Demetrio's neck and kissed his cheek.

"Thank you for talking to *mi marido*. It means . . ." He patted his chest. Demetrio understood.

"I like your husband," Demetrio said, and meant it.

Chenche grinned, kissed him again, and took off in his tiny swimsuit to clean up his club. As Demetrio watched, Chenche slipped his hand down the snug swimming trunks of the man sauntering beside him. The guy laughed. Chenche's hand settled in a very unsubtle way between the ass cheeks. Stefan seemed oblivious . . . or maybe to him it was no big deal.

I couldn't stand it . . . just couldn't stand it.

For a moment Demetrio stood feeling alone as the others left him behind, and it surprised him. He liked the rare moments he had to himself these days. He sometimes missed having a lover . . . a partner. He longed for the camaraderie of sharing his days and nights with someone special, someone who understood and supported his crazy, hectic schedule, but would settle for a long-distance romance if it didn't drive him crazy.

He heard somebody shouting his name from across the street and waved at another club owner who was planting fresh geraniums in window box displays on his terrace.

" *¡Hermoso dia!*" The guy yelled over to him.

Demetrio concurred, waving back. It was a beautiful day, so lovely he didn't feel like going straight back to the club. His apartment, in the building right next door to Club Dino, was perfectly fine. It was bright and sunny, but he hardly spent time there. He tended to sleep at other people's places and catnap at the club.

He walked on, taking in the local sites, surprised still by the green cross over a shop door that denoted a local chemist. On a trip to California, he'd learned the green cross denoted legal marijuana dispensaries. He grinned. Eivissa was so laid-back, so friendly . . . it was the kind of place where you could go out for dinner Wednesday night and not come home until Saturday. Somebody was always insisting you needn't go home—you could stay the night at their place. In the winter season, this was especially true. There was more time to socialize and eating and shagging were the two main island pursuits.

He stood on the hill, the air so clear he could see a plane take off overhead down at the *aeropuerto,* and smiled to himself. His date from the early morning was probably heading back to the mainland that very moment.

Outside an apartment terrace a block from Club Dino, he stared at the onetime home of one of the most famous local DJs on the island, Allister Logue. He was a colorful character on an island full of them. Demetrio shuddered when he thought about Allister. They'd met several times before Demetrio had moved to Eivissa, but Allister, one of the most dazzling people on the island, had somehow fallen on seriously hard times. He had returned to England last June, seeking fame and fortune. These two things were more important to Allister than fresh air or water.

He went back home, apparently broke and staying in homeless shelters. He applied to be a contestant on the series *Big Brother,* and when he was eliminated, sank into a deep depression. On July 24, with his passport and a suicide note in his pocket, he walked to Charing Cross station and threw himself under a moving train.

What disturbed Demetrio so much was that Allister never let on how lonely and diminished his life had become on Eivissa. He wasn't an easy personality, to be sure, but what had prompted such a gruesome suicide? His death was the subject of a lot of discussion when Demetrio moved to the island. Everybody wondered what they could have done to help him. Demetrio realized that in his lifetime, Allister had been fun but enigmatic. When his luck ran out, he probably hadn't reached out to anybody, hoping he could turn things around and change his losing streak.

That was the thing about luck. It could change. Demetrio frowned. Now that he was living here, the locals talked about Allister, but he was no longer a big, exotic bird on a small island. Demetrio shook off his gloomy thoughts as he realized new tenants had taken over Allister's digs. It was a new day and a new life. Demetrio had taken the plunge and moved to Eivissa. He wouldn't allow himself to isolate himself or to brood. No, he would mingle, mingle, *mingle.* He would treat every day as if life was a celebration.

He started checking off his to-do list in his mind. He needed to stock up on cheese and hors d'oeuvres before the evening crush. He recalled the last conversation he'd had with Allister, in which the older man had described himself as a freight train moving at high speed. "I'm no train. I don't mind a bumpy ride, but I want to enjoy it all. And I want to savor the time it takes to do it."

Demetrio forced himself to move past Allister's old digs, his heart twisting a little when he thought of Allister's little dog. They'd been inseparable, but not one person could tell him what had become of the little pooch.

He loved him so much. Maybe the little fella died. For a moment he paused. *I felt like that too when Ash left me. I'd loved him too. Except he was a man, not a dog.* Suddenly he really felt for Allister. Animals were better than people. They loved you unconditionally. They loved you regardless of your looks, your clothing, your stinky breath, or the money in your pocket.

That was the moment he came up with the idea for a memorial fundraiser for Allister. They'd put a little headstone in the churchyard right here in town. Burials and graveyards had a strong history here, where food was left for the *Lares*, the ancient Roman deities said to watch over the dead. Yes, before the summer became too crazy, he'd do it. That way whenever he became sad or lonely, he'd go visit Allister's memorial. Whatever the former promoter had been through here, he was a son of Eivissa, and Demetrio could feel the man's wild-child spirit on the wind.

Yes, he would honor his friend, but he would not follow in his footsteps. He wouldn't let sadness defeat him. Despite his good intentions, though, he did wonder about Ash. Big, bad Ash, so controlled by his penis he just had to push his way through the world with it in his hand . . . *Look at me!*

Demetrio applauded himself for not indulging in a bit of meaningless sex that morning. A good guy was worth the wait.

His thoughts were interrupted by a flurry of footsteps rushing past him and a lot of screaming coming from the beach. He turned to look, shading his eyes from the sun's glare with his hand. He'd forgotten his sunglasses down at the beach. That wasn't the only reason he went down there. He noticed a small speedboat capsizing in the sea. He began to run as he realized there was a man on board.

Demetrio watched Chenche and Stefan diving under the boat and bringing a man back up to the surface. The man wasn't moving. Demetrio pulled out his cell phone and wondered who to call. The police in Spain were different from all other places. There were several different branches of the force, even on the island. He could call the distress rescue service, but what if the man was already dead?

He ran down to the water's edge to see if he could help, aware only of the ferocious sunburn on the unconscious man's body as Chenche and Stefan dragged him out of the water and onto the sand.

CHAPTER TWO

Chenche was on his knees beside the prone man, his mouth clamped over the blue, lifeless lips.

Geez . . . the guy's half-dead and bloody Chenche can't keep his mouth off him!

Demetrio was surprised how well Stefan and Chenche worked as a team. Stefan pumped the guy's chest as he muttered into his cell phone in Spanish. Demetrio realized Stefan was receiving instructions from the distress rescue service. An ambulance was on its way. He stood around feeling useless as he and the other looky-loos watched Stefan and Chenche work on the strange man.

He came to life as if plugged into an invisible electrical source, coughing and spluttering up water.

Demetrio and the others watched helplessly as Chenche and Stefan turned the guy over, thumped his back, and water spilled out of his mouth.

Those watching burst into spontaneous applause. A few crass onlookers took photos of the guy with their cell phones. Demetrio watched the grin on Chenche's face. He brushed sand away from the guy's raised face. He spluttered more water and his eyes tried to open, but it looked like his eyelids were caked closed.

"Oh," the guy moaned. One eye had opened, and Chenche cradled the guy's head in his hands. *Imagine waking up to that golden boy kneeling on the sand beside you.*

The stranger's head lolled. Stefan and Chenche lifted him to his feet. Now that he was awake and more or less mobile, people took off, but Demetrio stayed as the ambulance arrived.

"What's your name?" Stefan asked the stranger in several languages.

No response.

The ambulance driver helped him onto a stretcher. The man lay back, his gaze from his one open eye resting on Chenche. The ambulance driver shoved him into the back of the old-fashioned van and drove away.

"That was lucky," Demetrio said.

Chenche nodded. "I think he swallowed much . . . water."

I bet he wants to swallow your cock, too. Demetrio shook the stupid, jealous thought from his head. Chenche and Stefan had saved the guy's life, but to them it seemed like no big deal. They hugged Demetrio good-bye. He went back to his club and they went to theirs. He watched them enter the club via the ground-level entrance. Their café and restaurant faced the beach. Their club took up the remaining two floors above it. Through the open windows, Demetrio could see the cleaning crew working on the floors and tables.

He sighed. As Stefan managed everything in his life effortlessly, Demetrio had inherited the world's worst cleaner, Jeanine, a forty-year-old American woman who'd come to Eivissa with hopes of a dancing career. She looked great and danced well, but youth was the prized commodity on the island, and men were the hottest dancers. She had apparently changed gears to become a psychic reader, er, spiritual adviser, yoga teacher, masseuse, and a cleaner.

She might have been good at her other jobs — rumor had it she was a moody spiritualist but a fantastic yogi — but she leaned on the cleaning gig for her regular income. And as a cleaner she was damned frightening. She broke things and didn't mention it and spent an inordinate amount of time on her cell phone. When he discovered it was because she was busy networking homes for the island's numerous stray and abandoned cats, his heart softened toward her. This was the endearing side to her. Besides, she got her work done eventually, and she was a cheery chick to have around.

Demetrio had come to enjoy her friendship. They frequently chatted about men and he'd coax her into forgetting about crushes on guys who were really gay. She should have been working on the 'other side' of the island, but she loved her sexy gay friends, and they her. When Demetrio learned she still got her period, he downloaded the Period Me app to his cell phone so he would have advanced warning of when to go easy on her, and when he wouldn't need to ply her with enormous slices of *pastel de chocolate y almendras*, the local specialty of chocolate almond cake.

Crash!

He hurried into the bar and he saw one of his wine glasses smashed on the antique Italian quarry tiles. She flashed him a guilty look and picked up a dustpan and broom, taking care of the mess as she kept up her conversation on her cell phone. "We have to rescue that colony," she said. "There's a momma kitty and five babies. I heard from a fisherman that somebody dumped a horseshoe whip snake right near that dock. Damned snakes!"

Snakes had become a huge problem on a few of the Balearic islands. The local cats were able to catch and kill some, but more and more snakes came as accidental stowaways on olive trees shipped via cargo hold to Eivissa. Residents were supposed to check tree roots for them and then report the reptiles to the Santa Eulalia police force, by calling 112. Frequently they dumped them in back alleys or by the seaport. There had been a legend that the island's ruling goddess, Tannit, had woven some magic spell over the natural red soil located here that repelled snakes. Of the four species that had found their way here, none had apparently heard of this legend and thrived.

Jeanine worried about her kitty friends and knew how to charm men. Whoever she spoke to, agreed to take on a family of five felines. If only she could be as persuasive yet gentle when dealing with men in her romantic life.

"I'll meet you there, don't you worry." She paused.

Demetrio tried to catch her eye. She was supposed to be cleaning.

"What's that?" she asked, then laughed. "Oh, you won't have any trouble finding me. In fact, I'd say I'm hard to miss."

That was true. She looked like a parrot in her long green dress, red shoes, and fire-engine red hair. Or as she called it, rocket fire.

She ended the call and glanced at Demetrio. "I'll only be a few minutes, I promise."

"Don't worry about it."

"Do we have any chocolate cake?" she asked, her tone hopeful.

With her lithe figure, he wondered where she put the copious amounts of sweets she ate. "One slice left from last night." He smiled. "Just for you."

She ran off like a little kid, and Demetrio examined his menu for the night's festivities. He'd organized a wine and cheese evening, with both components arriving that afternoon from the islands of Minorca and Majorca, which were two of the four main Balearic Islands, along with Eivissa and Formentera.

He checked his list. Half the wine had arrived, including four cases of the highly coveted 2004 Anima Negra Son Negre, a very intense yet elegant red wine from Majorca. He also had three cases of a stunning white wine direct from the Bodegas Herederos Rios vineyard, thanks to Stefan. The 2001 vintage was supposed to be the vineyard's best year. He was still waiting on several cases. He made some calls, checking on the boat delivery times, and then Jeanine returned, casually mentioning a box of cheese had just arrived from Minorca.

Demetrio almost flipped out when he saw the box sitting on the sink in the back bar, but he needn't have worried. It had all been beautifully packed in dry ice. Balearic cheeses were wonderful. He was pleased to see a huge variety in the container, including his favorite, the *Mahón*, a creamy soft cheese made from the milk of three different varieties of cows. There were also several *Tetilla* cheeses, the most unusual cheeses he had ever seen because the smoked domes looked like dunces' caps. In fact, that's what they were called on the islands: *Bufone*, the Spanish word for it.

He found several wheels of the local stinky blue cheese, and checked on his delivery of bread. His relationship with the staff of Espardel had become increasingly friendly since he'd started ordering all his baked goods from them. They rewarded him with breakfast rolls buñuelos, sweet choux pastries for his own personal breakfast each day.

Within minutes he'd received the status on all his deliveries, and he started to relax. He'd booked a pair of Spanish guitarists the previous week, and they'd proved so popular he'd booked them out for this week too. He knew they were anxious to visit the other islands, but he'd sweetened the deal with free accommodation in one of the small apartments the local club owners pitched in to pay for, free meals, and drinks when they played.

He checked over the club, liking what he saw. Jeanine followed him, a churlish look on her face. She hated being supervised, but left to her own devices, she overlooked many things such as comatose patrons slumped in the restrooms, paper towels, and soap. She also tended to take shortcuts in the cleaning process.

"Everything looks great," he told her, and noticed her visibly relaxing.

"Any chance I can work in the bar this weekend?" she asked.

He steeled himself against visibly cringing. She'd worked for years at the Troubadour in Los Angeles and mixed one hell of a drink, but she'd slept her way around the small island and tended to develop obsessions with men who became petrified of her. He'd tried talking to her about easing back on her compulsive nature where the club was concerned. She always said she understood but then turned right around and developed a new fixation on some poor, unsuspecting schmo who, nine times out of ten, bonked her in a drunken stupor and repented his actions almost immediately.

"I think we're set for this weekend," he lied. He had to lie. She'd bonked one of the Spanish guitarists, and she'd almost chased him out of the club just leering at him and sitting close to the stage when he performed. With her behind the bar, he'd be terrified.

"Are you sure?" She frowned.

Well, her eyebrows sort of wiggled. She'd had so much Botox and rubber cement injected into her forehead her skin and facial muscles did weird, unnatural things.

"I talked to José and Santana, and they said we were short two bartenders for Saturday night."

Bastards. I'll get 'em for this!

"No," he said. "I got two guys coming in from Sugar."

"Oh."

It seemed hard for her to hide her disappointment. She turned around, giving a couple of ineffective swipes at the bar top with her polishing cloth. He took the opportunity to sneak outside and send a text to Stefan, asking him for help with the weekend bartenders.

Stefan called him back immediately. "You have a few minutes?" he asked.

"Sure. Why?"

"The guy we rescued this morning . . . he's here. Well . . .

come over. Maybe you can help."

Demetrio ended the call, curious about all the mystery. With Jeanine prattling in his ear about vibes and muttering darkly, he gave her a wave and crossed the road. Stefan greeted him at the door, Bluetooth on one ear, a second cell phone at the other. He pointed over to the bar, where Chenche was giving the performance of his life tossing a vintage cocktail shaker into the air.

Seated in front of him, on a high-backed, iridescent-yellow stool that typified Sugar's seating style, was the man they'd rescued earlier.

When he turned to look at Demetrio, his eyes were a brilliant blue. They seemed troubled, bewildered even, yet they were astonishing. Demetrio wanted to dive right into them. He hadn't noticed before because the man's eyes had been half-closed, and he'd been in deep distress. Though he still bore the terrible sunburn, he seemed wide awake now. And, it was difficult not to notice, very handsome.

His dark hair was shoulder length and fell in wet tendrils across his face. He wore shorts and a T-shirt that didn't look new, so they must have been borrowed. He wore flip-flops on his feet.

"Hi," Demetrio said.

"Hello." The stranger's gaze traveled back to Chenche, who now poured the contents of his shaker over four brandy balloons laced with chipped ice. Demetrio recognized the yellowish hue and unmistakable scent of aniseed as the tasty but lethal local liqueur, *orujo de hierbas*.

Chenche slid a glass over to the stranger, who touched the stem with shaky fingers, then moved away again.

"Are you crazy?" Demetrio blurted. "That stuff will knock him out. He almost drowned!"

"He's fine," Chenche said, frowning at Demetrio. "He has amnesia, but the doctors say his memory could come back, and a little drink won't hurt." He leaned over the bar and tried to plant a kiss on the stranger's lips, but the man snapped his head back in a reflex action. Chenche's frown deepened.

"Hierbas is healing," he insisted. "He needs healing."

"Yes, it's a wonderful tonic," Stefan said, joining his lover behind the bar. "Maybe a little strong before lunch, *novio*." He gazed at their visitor. "Would you like a beer? Maybe some coffee?"

Silence.

"Do you drink tea? Maybe a soft drink?"

Chenche still held the gleam of lust in his eyes. No doubt he'd planned to soft soap the guy with a few drinks, then complete his, er . . . rehabilitation with his massive cock.

"I don't know." The stranger's voice was flat, but Demetrio detected an English accent. Before he could ask questions, the man said, "I don't know what I like. I don't remember. I can't remember anything. It's all so hazy."

"Does your head hurt?" Stefan asked.

"Not like it did at first. The doctors said I had a touch of sunstroke. I feel better since they gave me fluids and some water to drink. I have no broken bones. I just don't remember much."

"What do you remember?" Chenche asked.

The man shook his head. "Nothing." A beat. "Wait . . . . I do remember a plane, but I don't know when I was on it. And I remember a boat."

"Yes, it capsized," Chenche reminded him.

"No . . . I remember a bigger boat. A lot of people . . . God, this is so frustrating. I see little snapshots in my mind, and I try to grab onto them, and the images just vanish."

"It must be incredibly frustrating," Demetrio said. "But look, as far as I'm concerned, you're welcome to stay with me as long as you like."

"You can stay with us," Stefan said. "We have a room." He

gestured to Demetrio. "Or you can stay with our friend here. Take your time. Maybe it will all come back to you."

"Thank you," the man said. "I appreciate that."

"Would you like to try the hierbas?" Chenche asked. "It is very good. It will make you feel happy."

The guy shrugged. "I don't know. I suppose I could."

"He's got no money, no passport. The police took his fingerprints and the hospital released him to us. I thought since he is English, maybe you could talk to him."

Stefan slid a brandy balloon toward Demetrio, who picked it up and sniffed. Lord, he loved the smell. All four men clinked glasses. It was a little sad to see the watchful expression on the sea stranger's face. He sipped his drink only after Demetrio took a slug of his own.

"Not bad," the guy said. "It reminds me of . . ." Light came to his face, then fled again. "I can't remember."

"Do you know your name?" Chenche asked.

"No. I don't think . . ." The man hesitated. "No, I don't think so."

"What are we going to call you? We have to call you something," Stefan said. "The police contacted Interpol. It might take a few days. For now, I'm afraid you're stuck here."

"With us!" Chenche leered at the poor guy, who looked a bit frightened.

"Is there a name you like?" Stefan asked.

"I like the sea."

"I know!" Chenche snapped his fingers. "How about *Océano*? That's the Spanish name for the sea."

"That's a good name. I like it." The stranger took a little more of his drink. A few more sips and the poor bloody bastard would like anything and everything.

"Océano it is." Demetrio grinned at him. "You are very lucky these guys happened to find you when they did."

"I know. I mean . . . I have no idea what I was doing in that boat. I don't remember getting into it, or if I was alone."

Océano. He supposed he could live with the name, but he had a weird feeling his own was a lot less exotic. Was he Tom, Dick, or Harry?

Wait. Was he any of those names? He worried that he'd forgotten something important. A phone call. He could remember nothing. Flashes, snapshots of time burned in his memory, or maybe it was the sun. The relentless, terrible sun that had eaten at his skin, threatening to burn through his flesh.

He thought he had been shot. Adrift in the boat, he'd awoken at one point during a storm in so much pain he couldn't move. He was surprised he hadn't been shot when he could finally free a hand from underneath his sprawled body to check. He was certain he'd find a bullet hole and blood.

Instead he found the skin peeling from his body, his legs trembling. He could no longer tell if he was hot or cold.

Now he forced himself to think, to try to remember. He kept seeing a man pointing a gun at him. A dark room. The sudden explosion of gunfire.

Take that. Had somebody said it, or was it part of some terrible dream?

Call me. Call whom?

The three men around him kept talking, giving him sympathetic gazes and warm smiles. Except the one they called Chenche. Man, he had a shark-like personality under that killer body and white-hot smile.

I feel like he wants to sprinkle salt and pepper on me and have me for lunch.

His partner . . . what was his name? He seemed a lot more warm and real. He also seemed nervous. As though he couldn't believe this sex god was his. Maybe he was afraid the sex god would leave him.

"Stefan!" he shouted, pleased he remembered the guy's name.

But Stefan stared at him, expecting a question. Océano lapsed into silence and a wall of blackness. Dark, swamping clouds enveloped him, so tight and thick he thought he might not be able to breathe.

"Océano? You're British." Demetrio gently interrupted his thoughts. "Have you spent any time here on Eivissa?"

He spread his hands in a helpless gesture.

"Nothing seems familiar?"

Océano shook his head. "No."

"What about me? Do I look familiar?" Chenche asked.

Océano stared at him. "No. Why? Do you know me? Have we met before?" Why did this notion make him feel so panicked?

Tell no one. Call me. Take that. The words reverberated around the clouds in his mind.

"No, I would tell you if I did. But I'm well-known. I make movies."

"Really?" Océano didn't recognize him. Chenche looked pissed.

"Yes, really."

"I don't know if I've seen you, sorry."

"Are you gay?" Stefan asked.

"Am I . . ." He couldn't think. The only one he was even remotely attracted to was Demetrio. He seemed normal. Nice. A bit remote. *Does that make me gay?* He just couldn't remember. *Take that.* He felt so lame when he said, "Well, I don't know."

The color rose in his cheeks. It was worse than being at the mercy of the sun, but the others laughed, and not in an unkind way.

"You're not attracted to me?" Chenche asked, looking

aghast.

"Not really. But you make a nice drink."

Chenche laughed despite the slight. "I'll make you another one. We can have a little lunch, and then do you want to have a little siesta? We have a very nice bedroom upstairs." He wiggled his eyebrows suggestively.

Oh boy, he is incorrigible. Demetrio couldn't believe how hard Chenche worked to win over the handsome, troubled stranger. Demetrio thought they should leave the poor guy alone to some extended bedrest that didn't include bouncing on the end of Chenche's prodigious cock.

Océano stared at Chenche, a look of horror on his face.

"He means that we have a guestroom, very nice, with big windows," Stefan said quickly. "It gets a little noisy at night, but you'll get used to it."

"Thank you, that would be nice."

Demetrio watched Chenche blend another round of drinks, only this time only Chenche and Océano drank. Stefan was fielding calls and seemed to be in the middle of several big negotiations. When Demetrio eavesdropped, he realized people were calling to see if there was any legal challenge they could take up to combat the recent passing of an antismoking law in Ibiza.

The Balearic Business Federation, or CAEB, had protested on behalf of the hundreds of bar owners with the Spanish government, worried the new ban would mean a drop in sales. So far it hadn't. All the bar owners Demetrio knew merely asked their patrons to smoke outside on the terraces. Nobody had objected . . . yet.

"We don't have a complete ban," he heard Stefan saying on his phone. "Some places like California even ban smoking on some public streets."

Demetrio turned to check on his own bar across the road. No delivery trucks, but Jeanine seemed to be on an awfully long break, cigarette in hand at an outdoor table, her cell phone glued to her ear.

Chenche kept tossing questions at the handsome visitor as one of the waitresses brought several tapas to the bar. Sugar served some of the best little dishes in town.

They started with *boquerones*, marinated fresh anchovies, a staple in tapa bars across Spain. Soon little dishes on Sugar's trademark S-shaped plates started flying out of the kitchen.

The four men switched to mineral water, which they all happily guzzled.

"Oh, this is wonderful," Océano mumbled around a mouthful of the house specialty, a potato omelet. "What is in this that makes it so spicy but sweet?"

"Paprika." Chenche grinned. "It is my grandmother's recipe."

Océano stopped forking the fried delicacy for a moment. "Paprika. Is that a red spice?"

All the men nodded.

"For some reason it's ringing a bell. I wonder if I cook. I . . . oh Lordy, what's this?" He pointed his knife at a newly arrived dish containing *pulpo a la Gallega*, another local favorite. "Octopus?"

"Yes, and it is prepared with potatoes, olive oil, and coarse sea salt." Stefan took a healthy portion of it.

"All these potatoes, and yet you all have such good bodies. How do you stay in shape?"

"Sex," Chenche said.

"Exercise," Stefan and Demetrio said in unison.

"Sex," Chenche said again.

Océano laughed.

"I like to fuck and fuck and fuck." Chenche drained his cocktail.

"Yes." His lover rolled his eyes. "We know you do."

Since he had their attention and everyone seemed to be in a good mood, Demetrio brought up his idea for adding more flowers and plants for Allister's memorial.

"I love it," Chenche said. "We'll raise money. We can even make a little statue at the beach . . . maybe a bench with a tree, and put his name on it. I think he'd like people sitting on him."

They all laughed. Demetrio loved the idea of a useful memorial. They settled on the idea of a bench and planting a tree.

"Let's do it," Stefan said.

As the final dish of *montaditos* arrived, Océano seemed to wilt before their eyes as he took in the mountain of amazing-looking little open-faced sandwiches. These were a specialty of tapas bars too. Most of them charged patrons by the number of toothpicks left on their plates since the little creations were all held together by toothpicks, but in recent months it had become apparent that some patrons hid their toothpicks. Most bar owners kept count of the toothpicks themselves now to prevent such idiotic theft.

Demetrio kept trying to keep count, when really, he should be focusing on their exhausted guest. He switched off his business brain. Océano looked so sleepy it was pitiful. It was the booze, Demetrio was certain. Just as the man opened his mouth, probably to ask if he could lie down, house music started to blare from the speakers strategically placed all over the bar's three stories.

"Dance with me." Chenche held out a hand to Océano, who shook his head. He looked suddenly pale and very fragile.

"Are you okay?" Demetrio put his hand under the man's elbow.

Océano shook his head. "I can't stand this music. It makes me feel quite sick. Do you know someplace quiet where I could maybe lie down and rest my eyes? Please?" he implored.

"You can come to my place," Demetrio said. "I have to go back anyway. I'm waiting for a delivery."

The man looked relieved. "Oh wow, thanks." He reached beside him for a black plastic bag. "I have cream for my sunburn and some drops for my eyes from the hospital. They had to flush my eyes out. They still hurt like hell."

"Here, don't forget the sunglasses I gave you, and if you need more clothes, we have plenty," Stefan assured him.

"Thank you. I really appreciate it, and thanks for lunch. It's the best meal I ever ate . . . I think."

His disarming smile made them all laugh.

Chenche shook his head but blew him a kiss. "And still he walks away from me. Leave some for me, Demetrio."

Demetrio was mortified. Man, Chenche always had to go there.

He led Océano across the road.

"Salt and pepper. He wants me with salt and pepper," Océano muttered. He seemed fretful. That was understandable. He appeared to be shaking, too. Demetrio took his time, leading the man slowly toward Club Dino, where they found Jeanine laying out a spread of tarot cards on one of the outside tables.

She glanced up, saw the newcomer, sized him up instantly, and sprang to her feet.

"Well, hello, handsome," she said, dragging out the greeting.

"Jeanine, this is Océano. He's coming over for a little rest."

She smirked. "Is that what the kids are calling it these days?"

Demetrio's ears burned with embarrassment. "Come this way, Océano."

"Is everyone so sex mad here?" Océano asked, dropping his voice as they passed by her.

"It's worse in winter and spring. Not much else to do." De-metrio's attempt at humor failed. The man stared at him, a grave expression on his face. "Do you want to take a quick shower?"

"I had one at the hospital, thanks. I wouldn't mind some water, though."

"No problem. I'm sure you must be dehydrated after your journey."

"I guess." Océano sighed as they climbed the stairs to the second-floor rooms. He apologized. "I wish I could remember."

Demetrio understood. "My place isn't as fancy as Chenche's. It's really a crash pad, but the bed is pretty comfy."

"Anything's better than that damned boat. I have an idea I was in that thing for several days."

"You have bad sunburn, which would indicate that."

"I don't know." The man stood, leaning with his forehead pressed against a wall. "I'm so sick of hearing myself say that."

"Don't worry about it. Here's your room. I'm gonna throw on some sheets for you." He opened the windows and Océano peered outside.

"I'm so happy I washed up in such a lovely place. You're so very kind, Demetrio."

"Thanks." He found his guest a fresh towel in the small linen closet and put it over the back of a chair in the bedroom. He was surprised to see Océano already climbing into the bed.

"I'll go get you some water."

He wasn't gone long. By the time he came back, Océano was sleeping, snoring a little. Demetrio left the tray with the water and a glass on the chair with the towel, shut the door, and let the man sleep.

Back downstairs, Jeanine waylaid him. "That's the guy that

almost drowned?"

"Yes."

"I did a reading on him. I think he's escaped from prison somewhere. I think he's dangerous."

Oh God. "Listen, sweetie, I know you like bad boys, but this guy's had a rough time. He has amnesia. We're just taking care of him until he figures out who he is. So be nice and let him sleep, okay?"

"Okay." Her gaze traveled up the stairs. "Is he married?"

"No idea, sweetie."

"Is he straight? Is he gay?"

"Like I said, I have no idea. I don't think *he* even knows."

Anger flared in her eyes. "That's convenient. I'd hide the cash float if I were you." She turned and pretended to busy herself with some dusting.

Demetrio opened his mouth to protest. His cash registers all operated via computer and required passwords to open. Still, he'd been stiffed by one guy almost upon his arrival. He would just caution his staff to be vigilant. For a moment he thought about the man upstairs. Who was he?

He put a call through to the local police. There were so many branches on the island, and each took their functions very seriously. He was shunted from one department to another.

As it turned out, Océano, or Mister Nobody, as the police had taken to calling him, fell under the jurisdiction of the tourist police who patrolled the sea and airports and anything to do with tourism.

Finally speaking to Jaime Apolinar, the *alférez,* or second lieutenant, now in charge of the case, Demetrio was pleased the cop didn't seem too worried about the washed-ashore stranger.

"Can you come and see me?" the alférez asked. "The *comisaria de policia* is on Avinguda de la Pau. Do you know the big building with the mirrored windows that thinks it is a disco ball?"

"Er, yes."

"Well, we are right there on the main road between Can Misses Hospital and McDonald's. I will be waiting."

Demetrio hated to leave the club with his guest sleeping, alone and vulnerable, but his new kitchen hand, Luis, a Portuguese boxer struggling through an enforced medical suspension due to broken ribs, a broken nose, and two fractured fingers, waltzed in for a cup of coffee.

After quickly explaining the situation to Luis, Demetrio felt comfortable leaving the slim but hulking man in charge of their visitor.

He grabbed a taxi a few blocks away. The driver tried to tack on a port fee. Demetrio became incensed. This was a common ruse with drivers carrying passengers from the airport. This guy was crazy trying to pull off a stunt like that nowhere near the airport, and with a local, too.

"*¡Yo vivo aquí!* I live here!"

The driver gave him a surly look and plunged forward, driving so fast it seemed certain to Demetrio the driver wanted to get rid of him as fast as he could.

Outside the island's main police station, the driver squealed to a stop. Demetrio peeled off some euros and stepped outside. The car peeled away before he had a chance to close the door.

He gazed up at the blue-towered brick building. He'd visited here once when he lost his Alien Registration Card during a trip to the island the previous summer. He smiled as he approached the 'disco ball,' tamping down the urge to suddenly sing 'Lady Bump,' and entered the unique, ultramodern building.

A uniformed woman at the desk looked annoyed with his passable Spanish, or was it her sudden workload? A glance to his left showed two grim-faced guys sitting on a bench against the wall, handcuffed to two civil guards.

Demetrio guessed the men had been arrested for theft. The handcuffs could have been an indication that neither man had an NIE card on them. All foreigners were supposed to have an alien ID. Perhaps this situation was more dire. He didn't know what made him tiptoe to the bench beside them, but something made him want to keep quiet. He observed the posters warning female tourists to keep their purses safe. A cartoon image showed some guy on a dance floor gyrating as an unseen hand pilfered his wallet from his back pocket.

That was Ibiza for you. Crime accompanied the wave of tourists. Petty theft and drugs were the biggest crimes.

"Sr. Reyes?"

"Alférez Apolinar?" He looked up to see the second lieutenant, a burly man with a ready smile.

"Please, I insist, call me Jaime," the second lieutenant said, leading the way to his office. He spoke very good English, which helped the flow of conversation.

Inside the slightly warm office, Demetrio accepted the generous offer of a bottle of mineral water. He snapped the cap, drinking deeply as Jaime perched on a corner of his desk, leaning toward him, outlining what he knew. He, too, had a bottle of water in his grip and, talking with his hands, shed a drop or two of liquid on Demetrio's face.

"We have learned that the boat Océano was on is registered to a British businessman named Philip Gordon. Have you ever heard of him?"

Demetrio shook his head.

"We asked Mister Nobody if that was his name. He said he didn't know. He let us take fingerprints, so that was a good sign he wasn't trying to hide anything." He lifted his shoulders in an expressive way.

Demetrio hesitated before asking, but he really wanted to

know.

"Do you think he really has amnesia?"

"I don't know. He seemed sincere to me. I haven't met an amnesiac before, but the two doctors who treated him tell me they think it is legitimate. He was in bad shape, you know, sunburned, dehydrated. I think he has suffered some kind of shock."

"One of my staff members thinks he might be a prison escapee."

Jaime laughed. "Oh, just like the movies! Well, there has been nothing reported. Not from any Spanish jails, but I have sent out bulletins. We have his photograph circulating, but so far nobody remembers seeing him coming to any local airports. We have customs and immigration officers running through their security footage all over the country.

"We'll know more when we get his fingerprints back, hopefully. I know they took blood from him at the hospital, but that was more for health reasons than for identification."

"Can you use it for DNA?"

"Yes. Mister Nobody gave us permission. He has been very cooperative. That pleases me."

"Well, I appreciate you talking to me," Demetrio said, getting up to leave.

"It's no problem. So, he's staying with you?"

"For now."

"And what is the best number for us to reach you in case we need to contact you or Mister Nobody?"

Demetrio gave Jaime all his contact details.

"I don't think he's a violent man, not from what I saw, but you never know." Jaime shrugged again. "Just be careful, huh?"

"I will. May I ask . . . why did you pick Mister Nobody for his name?"

"Oh, in police circles, there is a famous case of a man who

turned up at a hospital in Toronto, Canada, saying he'd been the victim of an attack and had no memory of who he was."

"What happened to him?"

Jaime cleared his throat and moved off his desk. "He led the Canadian authorities on a big chase for some years. They couldn't decide if he was really amnesiac or if he was a fraud."

"Which was it?"

"He was a fraud, but it took a lot of years to prove it and he hurt a lot of people who tried to be kind."

People like me, Stefan, and Chenche.

"There are certain similarities here that are hard to ignore."

"What similarities?"

Jaime paused, reaching for the door handle. "Since the man is staying with you, I don't mind telling you, but I have to ask you to please refrain from talking publicly about this. That means no reporters . . . no strangers who ask questions in the bar."

"Understood."

"Mister Nobody showed up at the hospital in Toronto speaking in a perfect British accent like our friend here. He convinced a lot of people he'd lost his memory and people took him in. They looked after him. It took a long time, but they finally found out who he really was. He wasn't even British. He was Romanian. A Romanian imposter."

Oh boy.

"Does that mean you think *our* Mister Nobody is a fraud?"

"Oh no. It just means that we don't know." Again with the shrug. He opened the door and gave Demetrio a funny little bow. "Now that you tell me you and your friends have picked a name for him, we can release it to the media. Océano is a very good name, better than Mister Nobody. People will like that. He is a good-looking guy. Somebody must be missing him somewhere."

"Right." *Like a wife. Why does that thought bother me so much?*

"We have his picture going all over Spain and to other

parts of Europe. I hope we get something on him through fingerprints. He says he is open to cognitive therapy, not that we have much access to it here on the islands, but we could get him help in Barcelona or Madrid. He seems very willing to do everything we've suggested, but in the meantime, you be careful. We really don't know who the hell this guy is. He seems okay. He seems nice. But remember, who knows what those big, blue eyes are hiding?"

CHAPTER THREE

Océano opened his eyes and almost fell off the bed. A tall, thin guy with a bent, broken nose, two black eyes, and the fiercest scowl he'd ever seen was standing at the foot of his bed watching him sleep.

The stranger kept up the intense glare as he sipped at a shot glass of some clear amber liquid. Man. Even his fingers were broken.

Océano watched the guy sip and grimace a couple of times. He held up his fore and middle fingers, bandaged together and bound by splints.

"*Duele*." The man pulled a face.

"Ah. Pain. I have something that might help you." Océano struggled to rise, dizziness stopping him for a moment. Bright afternoon sun peeked around the edges of the bamboo slats in the blinds, a faint breeze wafting into the room.

He reached for the plastic bag they'd given him at the hospital and hunted for the pain meds. The entire foil packet was empty. He glanced over at the man with the black eyes. The guy looked at the floor, guilt flushing his features.

"Océano." He pointed to himself and looked inquiringly at the man whose gaze flickered around the room. "You?"

"Luis."

"Ah. Okay. Good." *What am I saying? Why is that good? What if he came here to assault me? Do I know him?* He jumped when the apparently beaten Luis put the shot glass on a chest of drawers and pulled a wallet from his pocket.

Thank God it's not a gun. Man, why do I think everybody wants to shoot me?

Because somebody did.

He was certain of it now but had no wounds to prove it. He kept seeing himself fall backward, tumbling into the sea.

How did I wind up on the boat?

Nothing. He had nothing. No memory after being shot. But the hospital staff insisted he had no bullet wounds.

He kept staring at Luis and suddenly remembered a name. He pointed at him. "*El Gallo.*"

Luis's face lit up. "Sí. ¡Sí!"

He took a carefully folded piece of paper from his wallet and handed it over to Océano, who opened it. An image of Luis in boxing gloves and a bloody pair of shorts greeted him. Luis was taking a face-altering punch from another man. Ah. That explained it. Luis was a boxer. *But how do I know his name?* El Gallo. The rooster. He scrutinized the page but couldn't read the words. He deduced that much, though. The man had lost his belt and had taken a severe beating in a boxing match. His gaze returned to the words. He could pick out the odd one here and there. It wasn't Spanish. For some reason he was aware that he could speak that language, but not this.

Lisbon. The word was printed at the top of the page. Lisbon was in . . . Portugal. *Okay. I can remember that. Why can't I remember my name?*

He got a sudden image in his mind of a bird crying out, of a tropical squall. *Was I on a boat? I have a feeling I am damned lucky to be alive.*

Luis caught his gaze.

Océano stared at the man's black cord slung around his neck. A luminous green plastic penis about an inch long hung from it. That made a statement for sure.

"¿*Café?*" Luis mimed sipping a drink.

"Yes. Sí. Thank you." Océano tried to rise. His stomach roiled. He hung on to the bedpost, afraid he'd fall face first to the floor. Luis rushed over and grabbed hold of him. Though Océano was wearing underpants and borrowed shorts, he felt naked and exposed as the other man put his arm around him, holding him steady.

A memory flooded the clouds lurking in his mind. Fear. Panic. Who to trust? Voices whispered. *Take that.* Gun shots. A trap. Yes. A tall man had helped him. Or had he? *Call me.* The words went round and round. He wanted to scream.

We were ambushed. But who was *we?* Sweat beaded on Océano's face and neck. It felt clammy under the weight of the well-intentioned man beside him.

The doctors had told him the waves of nausea and shaking were lingering seasickness. They'd given him medicine for it. He pointed a quivering finger at the plastic bag full of pills.

Luis snatched it and handed it to him with his free arm. Océano rifled through it, pulling out the package of Meclizine.

"Water," he gasped. His glass was empty, so they traipsed downstairs, Luis keeping his arm around him. In the kitchen, Luis hunted for a bottle of water. Océano couldn't wait and turned on the cold water tap in the sink. He stuck his head beneath the faucet and turned it on, gagging when the water turned out to taste salty.

"No, no." Luis looked horrified.

Océano kept spitting in the sink. It was horrible, truly the worst thing he'd ever tasted in his life. *I think.* He wiped his mouth with the back of his hand, hoping he wouldn't throw up. His stomach felt awful. Demetrio chose that moment to show up, concern etching his features as Luis talked in rapid-fire Spanish to him.

Demetrio gave Océano a sympathetic gaze.

"What the—is the water always so awful?"

"I'm afraid so." Demetrio's expression turned rueful. "It's always been like that on the island. A few places close to the new water mains have better water, but it's still not very tasty. Don't even attempt to boil it for tea or coffee. Drink bottled water only."

Océano nodded. He took the Pellegrino Demetrio slid across the bar top toward him, undid the lid, and began to drink. The smell of coffee improved his spirits. He downed a couple of pills, aware that Demetrio was watching him.

"What?" he asked, peeling another pill from the foil pack. He'd just realized when he'd taken a shower earlier, he'd swallowed great mouthfuls of water. Maybe that was why his stomach felt so bad.

Demetrio smiled at him. "Nothing. I just remember my first days in the island. I thought I'd landed on another planet."

Océano took a seat beside Demetrio at the bar. "But still you fell in love with the place?"

"Oh yes." Demetrio's gaze drifted out of the window toward the sound of laughter.

"What did it for you?"

Demetrio shrugged, returning his attention to Luis and Océano again.

Luis poured milk and foam into a cup of steaming coffee and handed it to Demetrio. He pointed to Océano and the milk jug.

"*¿Leche?*" he asked.

Océano nodded. "Yes. Sí. Please." He waited for Demetrio to answer his question.

"I took a walk one day up in the orchards. Very few visitors even know about them. But anyway, I could smell this delicious scent. It drove me crazy. I had no idea what it was, and I followed my nose until I entered this grove of trees filled with the most fragrant white flowers. I have never smelled anything like them in my life."

"What were they?" Océano sipped his water again.

"Almond blossoms." He shook his head, stirring his coffee. "And that, my friend, is Eivissa, one unexpected miracle after another. You take a walk and there is a little bit of sparkle. Somewhere, some way. It sneaks up on you, this island. Once she opens herself up to you, she doesn't let go. And those magical moments happen each and every day."

Océano liked the idea of a bit of magic. He liked the idea of fragrant white blossoms and sparkles in the sun.

He didn't know why the sudden thought of fear and panic was the next thing in his mind . . . as though good things, those small moments, were meant for those other than him.

With Eivissa being a small island, news had traveled fast. By the first crush of evening revelers, everyone knew Océano was staying with Demetrio, and the bar was packed with people wanting to meet the guy and take their photos with him. Demetrio was embarrassed. People's insensitivity never ceased to amaze him.

He found a pair of jeans, a shirt, some shoes, and socks, and urged the guy to take his time and get ready for the evening. He wanted Océano to relax, maybe have a glass of wine and have an early night. Instead he stood by feeling helpless as he watched his guest, who'd slept most of the afternoon away, brighten up long enough to pose for photos with dozens of girls who wanted to post the results on their Facebook and Flickr pages.

"You never know, somebody might recognize him," was the common refrain.

A few groups of guys wanted their pictures taken with him, too.

"This'll make my boyfriend back home *so* jealous," one of the guys said.

Demetrio kept a watchful eye on Océano, who seemed very

good-natured and sociable. Interestingly, he was no more responsive to the women trying to maul him as he'd been to Chenche. He didn't seem to like being stroked and pawed — by anybody. And lots of them tried.

He left at one point with a group of men, returning to report with awe about the crazy gay bars he'd visited. He leaned across the bar as Demetrio poured a couple of shots of cognac for two customers.

"Miss me?" Océano shouted.

"Hugely. You having fun?"

"Yeah. And learning heaps. So this is the gay section and it's called *Sa Pensa*, right?"

Demetrio laughed above the noise of the bar.

"I can't believe how tame your place is in comparison with some of the others I just saw."

"Where did you go?"

"Club Nonsense. Oh my God. The lava lamps and glittery disco ball were like something out of a bad John Travolta movie. I liked Dome, though. The transvestites were gorgeous."

Demetrio grinned.

"You got any coffee?"

"I've got a fresh pot right here." He reached to the coffee maker behind him.

"I'm interested in architecture," Océano told Demetrio, grabbing a stool at the bar as Demetrio poured him a cup of coffee. "I seemed to know a lot about it, and I have a terrible feeling it could be my chief occupation, apart from eating."

Demetrio laughed over the dueling Spanish guitars.

"I like this music. Better than the rubbish they play over at Sugar," Océano said.

"Hey, those guys saved your life."

"Yeah, I know they did. Sorry. I'm grateful, really I am. I just wish they had better taste in music. Say, doesn't the sound drifting over here bother you?"

Demetrio shook his head. "I'm used to it, and besides, the customers like the blend of sounds. They seem to dance to all of it at once."

"I noticed that. They love your wine and cheese, by the way." He looked over his shoulder. "Why does that girl Jeanine keep staring at me? She's a little . . . intimidating."

"I'll speak to her."

"Thank you. She keeps hitting on me, then gets mad when I tell her I can't go out with her. I don't mean to be rude, but until I can figure out who I am and how I came to be here, I feel I am useless to anybody. I can't get involved. What if I have a wife and child back home?"

"Do you think you have a wife and child?"

"No. You're going to get awfully sick of hearing me say this, but I just don't know. The good news is that I like you. I like being here and I'm relieved you're such a nice guy. You're the only guy I've met who doesn't have an agenda. It's very comforting." He drained his coffee. "That was nice, but it killed my buzz."

Man, this guy is all over the place.

"Would you like some wine?"

"What's the best wine you have?"

Demetrio pointed to two bottles on a tray on the bar.

"These are excellent. Want to try the red?"

"Yes, I think I do, thanks."

Demetrio poured him a glass. Emboldened by Océano's compliments, he had no problem shooing away pesky customers who made a beeline for the man. There were even two lesbian German tourists making a play for him. This was especially shocking to Demetrio. Sonja and Margita had shocked all the local bar owners by showing up a month ago and living rough in a toilet block at a local park. They'd been sleeping in the ladies' toilet each night, hanging out at the park and nearby beaches each day.

Nobody had realized they were homeless at first, and once they did, the bar owners pooled their resources, found the girls a room for nominal rent and jobs waiting tables by day. Now they wanted Océano to come and share their bed.

"We don't usually like men, but you have beautiful eyes," Sonja told him. "I would love you to make Margita pregnant."

Océano almost dropped his wineglass.

Help me, he mouthed to Demetrio.

Instantly Demetrio stepped into the conversation. "Océano, you mind coming outside to help me for a moment?"

"No." He looked distracted.

Demetrio gestured to his wait staff. "Won't be long. Everything okay?" he asked as they went out and stood on one of the terraces. Océano's attention focused on the festivities across the narrow street.

"I . . . do you mind if I smoke? I have a craving for a cigarette. Damn . . . I can't buy any. I can't even pay for this wine." Tears filled his eyes as he stared at Demetrio. "God, I hope I'm not always going to be this way."

Demetrio's heart ached for the man who left the terrace, drink in hand. Demetrio bummed a cigarette from one of the revelers crushing the cascade of outdoor terraces at Sugar.

Jeanine made her way to him, pausing to pump up her breasts in her already revealing skimpy top. When she was certain she'd achieved the desired amount of cleavage— somewhere near her chin—she advanced on the poor guy.

Océano saw her coming and almost choked on his cigarette. Demetrio would have intervened except he had a small crisis on his hands—free drinks for the musicians meant they'd been imbibing all night.

"They've been playing the same cords all night," a customer complained. "Once they've mastered the actual bloody song, I'll be back."

He slammed his glass on the bar and strode away from the

club, a group of men following him. They were laughing and joking, but it wasn't funny to Demetrio, who realized the two musicians were dead drunk and not playing much of anything.

Demetrio caught the eye of one of his bartenders, who instantly switched on the canned music. It was a great mix by one of the local DJs, and the absence of the recently departed men only meant some room was freed up at the bar. The two Spanish guitarists kept strumming, looking bleary-eyed. Had they not noticed they'd been replaced?

Suddenly Stefan was at his side. "Problems?"

Demetrio gestured at the two men. "Drunk."

Stefan's build and sterling reputation as a muscle man came to the fore. Within seconds he'd turfed out the musicians, telling them to sleep it off, and one of the DJs from Sugar took up the space on the dance floor. With two half-naked men now dancing beside Demetrio, the mood went from mellow to crazy. Money flowed into the bar. Demetrio sighed. Yes, it was nice, but he really loved the more gentle side of things.

"I owe you so many favors," he told Stefan, who clamped a hand to his shoulder.

"You would do the same for me. I have to go. My husband is dancing naked on the bar. He's wearing nothing but boots." The two men exchanged looks and laughed. Demetrio knew that within minutes, those boots would be stuffed with cash.

A few guys in the bar overheard and ran across the road. Some of them knew the gay-porn star Juan-Juan had a real name, but to them, Chenche would always be Juan-Juan.

Demetrio felt a hand at his elbow. Océano stood beside him, looking stricken.

"I can't read your menu. My God. I think something's wrong with my brain. I mean, really wrong."

Demetrio glanced at the page. "It's in Spanish. Try turning

it over."

Océano did as Demetrio suggested. He began to squint. "Well, I can read it, but I think maybe I usually wear glasses. I had trouble reading something Luis showed me earlier too."

Glasses. Where the hell would they find reading glasses this time of night?

He remembered this was Ibiza. You could always find whatever you needed someplace on the island.

"There's a chemist down the road. Come on, I'll take you." Jeanine joined them as they walked. She prattled on about music and math . . . trying to hit on anything that might jog Océano's memory. "Do you like animals?" she ventured.

"Can't you make her stop?" Océano whispered as they walked inside the chemist. They stopped to examine the cheap reading glasses on a display carousel just inside the door. Océano picked out a pair of black-framed glasses that made him look sexy and serious. He stared into the small mirror in the middle of the carousel. "Oh, this is better. I can even read the fine print. I think I'm also going to need a toothbrush."

Demetrio nodded. "Get what you need. Deodorant, shampoo, whatever."

Océano wasn't shy about loading up on toiletries and seemed to gravitate toward the British line of products. Demetrio paid, grinning to himself as he watched Océano reading the small print on a shampoo bottle as they walked back to the bar.

"I feel like I got my eyes back . . . but, you know, I wonder what happened to my glasses . . . . What happened to my life?"

"Would you like me to give you a psychic reading?" Jeanine asked as she broke into one of the many candy bars she'd purchased.

"No."

"It would help. I'm quite psychic, you know."

"No, you're not." Océano looked angry.

"What are you afraid of?" she asked, her tone accusatory.

"I'm not afraid of anything." Océano's voice rose. "But so far, you've suggested I'm an escaped convict, a wife killer . . ." a dramatic pause. "A member of the aristocracy who fell out of his castle window . . . and an escaped mental patient."

She pointed a finger at him. "That's my favorite theory."

"All right, all right. Jeanine, leave Océano alone." Demetrio had a few complaints about her impromptu readings. She mostly predicted fame and good fortune, but something about Océano had stirred up her urge for trouble. "At least you haven't picked up on him being a cat killer."

"He's so grumpy. All the handsome ones are." She shook her head in a mournful way.

Océano gaped at her. "You think I'm handsome?"

"Yes."

"But grumpy."

"Yes."

"Sorry." He shrugged.

Jeanine gave him a sweet smile that seemed like the sun after a flash rainfall. "That's okay. You've been through a lot." She pushed her shades from the top of her head back down over her eyes. "I've got feral cats to feed." She gave them a finger wave and rushed off down the street.

"What a character," Oceano said.

"That's what I always say." Demetrio checked his watch. "You hungry?" he asked as they squeezed their way into the Sugar bar. He grinned at the sight of a gyrating Chenche on the dance floor, naked in knee-high black boots, dancing to Ellen Allien's *Dust Remixes*. The crowd was going wild. Stefan knelt beside him, scooping up bills as people tossed them. Chenche rubbed his crotch in a few happy faces.

A few adventurous guys tried to suck him, but Chenche

was quick to swivel his hips away. It just got him bigger tips.

Demetrio was surprised when Stefan turned to him, pressing a wad of crumpled notes in his hand. "For Allister," he shouted in Demetrio's ear. "I'll let you arrange everything. We loved him too, you know."

It was after three o'clock when Demetrio finally made it back to Club Dino. He turned off the music and closed up the bar. His bartenders had stacked the dishwashers with the last remaining glasses and drifted off to Sugar, where music still pounded out of its open doors. Demetrio turned off the lights on his two outdoor terraces and closed and locked the wrought-iron gate. A few latecomers yelled for entry from out front, but he was forced by law to ignore them.

Only his lone guest, Océano, remained, sitting on a stool, eating his third slice of tiramisu pie.

"I want you to add up everything I've eaten so I can pay you back," Océano insisted. "You have the best food here."

"Thanks."

"No, I mean it. And I want to repay you. You've been so kind."

A beat.

"How can you stand that music? Can you sleep through the noise?"

"Yes." Demetrio finally smiled. "I don't live here. I live down near the beach. It's much quieter there."

Demetrio was too tired to care at this point about what the guy had or hadn't eaten . . . but he noticed Océano had made himself at home, enjoying everything Club Dino had to offer. Demetrio wordlessly put chairs on the tables and swept the floor. Everything else was clean. He turned to Océano.

"Will you be okay here?"

"No, I won't. That bloody music is deafening. Can't I come home with you?"

Demetrio scratched his chin. He never invited anybody back to his private digs.

"Okay," he said. "But it's a sofa bed. Hope you'll be comfortable."

"Anything it better than this racket. Just let me get my stuff."

Océano shuffled away, licking his fork. When he returned, he dropped the fork next to his plate, leaving it on the bar. Demetrio felt a little tweaked about this. Hadn't the guy noticed he and the others had been cleaning for the last hour? Who did he think was going to clean up after him?

Maybe he was used to being waited on hand and foot. Maybe he *was* an aristocrat who'd fallen out of a castle window, like Jeanine thought. Demetrio brushed the thought aside.

"We clean up after ourselves here, Océano. Do me a favor please and put your dish in the sink."

"Oh."

Demetrio watched as Océano walked behind the counter to put the dish in the sink.

"The fork, too, please." He was feeling thoroughly exasperated by this guy.

"Oh. Why didn't you say so?" Océano reached for the fork and deposited it with a clatter into the sink.

Don't say anything. Just count to ten . . .

"I hope your place is a lot quieter than this," Océano said.

Demetrio just nodded. They slipped out the backdoor into the alley, where he checked up and down to make sure they were alone. He'd been jumped once and didn't care to repeat the experience. The man who'd attacked him was drunk and looking for spare cash. He shuddered now, thinking about it. He dropped the garbage he'd carried out into a bin and kept moving. Océano trotted to keep up with him.

Eivissa had its share of hardened partiers. The one thing it didn't have was poverty or major crime. There were no panhandlers and no homeless people. It made a nice change from London.

Océano shuffled along in his borrowed shoes. They were clearly too big for him. They'd buy more tomorrow. They followed the well-worn path of tiny, twisting roads created long before there was even a notion of motor cars. Consequently, most of the old town was only navigable by foot, motorbike, or bicycle. Bicycles were tough thanks to the tortuous hills, but once you were outside of the city, you could drive a car, especially in the northern hilly sections.

"This is it," he said, unlatching the gate to the little beach bungalow in a smart triplex he'd bought along with the bar from Dino. It was small, cozy, and perfect for one.

"Say, this is smashing," Océano said. "Got anything to eat in the fridge?"

Demetrio couldn't help quirking an eyebrow at the guy. Océano hadn't stopped eating since they'd had lunch at the bar.

Océano caught the look. "Don't understand it, but I'm famished. Hey, can I have this popcorn?"

Demetrio shrugged. Popcorn was easy to replace. He opened up the sofa bed, threw some fresh sheets and a duvet on it, and gave him a couple of pillows.

"I'm turning in. Bathroom's this way." He pointed down the hall. "I sleep until about ten, so please try to keep it down until then, okay?"

"Sure. No problem."

Demetrio had his own tiny bathroom off his bedroom. He showered quickly, then brushed his teeth and rejoiced in his cool, clean sheets as he slid between them. He usually slept in the buff and debated putting on something. Fuck it. He always slept better naked. His head hit the pillow, and he was just drifting off when he heard his bedroom door opening.

"Are you asleep?" Océano shuffled in and peered down at

him.

"Almost. What's up? Why are you still wearing those shoes?" Demetrio couldn't keep the testiness out of his tone.

"My feet hurt. And now it's too quiet. Can I sleep with you?"

"Jesus Christ, Goldilocks. I'm trying to get some rest here."

"Me, too." Océano ran around the side of the bed, kicked off his shoes, and got in beside him.

Man, oh man. Why me? Why did I say he could come and stay? Technically speaking I only agreed for him to have a siesta at the club. I didn't realize I was signing on to be his full-time nursemaid.

He turned his back against Océano, surprised when the guy scooted closer to him. *Shit, he's naked!* The man had started spooning him. *How the fuck am I supposed to sleep?* He was even more stunned when Océano snaked his hand around Demetrio's body and rested it lightly on his warm, flat belly. Demetrio felt his cock getting hard and bouncing against the back of the other man's hand.

Shit! Fuck! Arrrghh!

Océano seemed oblivious. Within seconds he was asleep, his soft breath on the back of Demetrio's shoulders and neck. And Demetrio was in torment.

Shut your eyes, fool. And go to sleep.

But sleep eluded him. Something about the whole episode troubled him. Then he remembered. When he was nineteen, his older cousin John had gone to Australia backpacking with his new bride, Stella. They'd sent back postcards to their family members in England. They loved the bushland and had secured work visas for twelve months. John had taken a desk job as a park ranger for the Wildlife Service in Sydney. He apparently had problems with his supervisor. Since he'd heard all of this third hand, the details were sketchy, but Stella soon called John's family saying he had disappeared.

It had been a shock to all of them. Demetrio, his father, and John's two brothers had all gone out to Australia to help look for him. John Reyes's disappearance had made front-page news. The facts were mysterious. He'd told his boss he was going to lunch but didn't take his wallet, which was found in his desk drawer with his money and bank card still in it. His bank account was not touched from that day.

Somehow somebody recognized him and claimed to have seen him on a northbound train, crossing the street and darting into the bushy parkland at the end of the railway line. It was an old woman who the police said made frequent calls to them with other nonsensical reports. John's family members invaded the park, which was scary and dark at night. They searched and searched and went home, dismayed and emptyhanded.

Twelve months later his burned skeletal remains were found not far from where they'd looked and almost a mile deep into the bush where the old lady said she'd seen him. He would never have been found if it hadn't been for wildfires raging in the forest. Emergency crews went out there, and during their tamping of the flames, found the skeleton lying on the ground. Identified later as John Reyes, his human remains still wore his work uniform, and one arm was slung above his head. The coroner could give no certain cause of death due to the condition of his body.

What happened to John? Sometimes, just sometimes, Demetrio recalled how frightening that bushy parkland was. Had John survived long? What made him flee? Had he been afraid of the dark? Tears pricked the back of his eyes. What random fate was it that allowed Océano to survive but John to die?

He listened to the slow, steady breathing of the man huddled against him. He got the feeling it wasn't sexual comfort, but sheer human warmth Océano sought. Demetrio wasn't used to sleeping with somebody all night. He tended to have sex and go on his merry way. He fought to ignore the deep breathing in his ear and to focus on the sound of the ocean near his building. Soon it lulled him to sleep.

Morning came hot and fast. Too fast. From somewhere he heard wild laughter and sat up in bed. Océano wasn't with him. He could hear him in the living room, talking. Frowning, Demetrio threw on clothing and cast his glance toward the clock radio. Eight o'clock. He'd asked Océano to keep the noise down until ten, but as he stormed into the kitchen, he was surprised to find the noise was coming from the radio and that Océano was cooking.

"I'm making breakfast. I found some money in your cookie jar and went to the store. I hope you like eggs. Yes, you do like eggs. I remember now. We had an omelet yesterday. Coffee?" He held up the pot, lifting it off the stove.

It was hard to be mad at a guy who was an obvious whiz in the kitchen.

"Sure." He grabbed a chair at the table and watched Océano pour him a cup. Demetrio reached for the milk in the fridge.

"What else do you remember?"

"I put some in the milk jug. You want sugar?" When Demetrio shook his head, Océano shrugged.

"Don't remember much, but I think I jumped from somewhere and really banged my feet. Look."

Demetrio glanced down and noticed the man's feet were black and blue and swollen.

"My God . . . you've sprained them."

"That would explain why they fucking ache. After breakfast, I'm going back to the hospital. My right nostril hurts like a motherfucker too."

"Sorry to hear that. I'd drive you, but my car's been in the shop for days. I've had transmission trouble with it for weeks now. The salt air here kills everything. Cars, dishwashers, dryers, water pipes . . . ."

"That's no problem. Stefan said he'd take me. He mentioned your car. He says you bought a lemon."

"You talked to Stefan about my car?"

"He called to check on me. He called your cell phone. I tried to wake you but you're a hard guy to wake up."

"Not normally."

"You snore, too."

Demetrio frowned. "No, I don't."

"Have it your way, but I heard you all night. You snore."

Jesus . . . how come nobody ever mentioned it before? Maybe because I don't do sleepovers . . . .

Océano plated their eggs and deposited slices of fresh bread on the edge of the dishes.

"I hope it tastes okay. I cooked from memory. Or instinct. I guess. I felt inclined to cook in volume. I wonder if I'm used to cooking for large numbers of people."

In prison, maybe. Or the armed services. "How many eggs did you use?"

"A dozen."

A dozen? Hello, cholesterol! Demetrio said nothing. The eggs were very good.

"Maybe you're married and you have a lot of children."

"I don't think so. I seem to . . . find children irritating. I kinda like that there aren't many on the island." He sat down and winced. "Nice to take the weight off my feet."

"You should keep them elevated."

"Probably. I'm full of aches and pains today. My back aches. Wait . . . maybe you can tell me. Do I have any bruises on my back?"

He stood and turned, whipping his T-shirt over his head. Demetrio was stunned by the purple bruises on the man's back.

"You know, you fell overboard when your boat capsized. Maybe you got hit by the boat. And don't forget you had

Stefan and Chenche working on you with CPR."

"Oh yeah, that's right." He shrugged. "I still want to go back to the hospital, though. It hurts when I breathe in."

Demetrio felt bad for the guy, but soon they heard a honking sound out front.

"That'll be Stefan." Océano glanced at the readout on Demetrio's cell phone. When Demetrio's cell phone rang, Océano took the call. Clearly, he'd commandeered it. "Yep, it's him." With a cheery wave, he got to his feet. "Oof . . . that hurts. Say, you got a spare key you can give me?"

Demetrio nodded, fishing in his utility drawer for one. It had a tennis racket key ring attached to it. A strange look crossed Océano's face as he took possession of it.

"I love tennis. How odd . . . I remember playing a game. In the rain." He shook his head, as if trying to discard the memories. "I don't know. I remember such random stuff. You play?"

"All the time."

"We'll have to have a game." He looked out the window. "He's on a motorbike. Man, I wonder if I've ever been on one of those before?"

He scratched his head, deep in thought. And with that he was gone, leaving Demetrio with the dirty dishes. He washed them, having the final half cup of coffee in the pot. He made himself a fresh batch, realizing it was nice to have somebody in his home. Yes, even if he was a guy without a name and without real memories . . . .

But I can help him. I never got to help John. Or Allister.

He realized it had been a long time since he'd spoken to John's widow, Stella. She'd never remarried. In the fifteen years since her husband's passing, she'd lived a very quiet life in the British countryside with her garden and wild birds. He checked the time. He'd call her. Cradling the cell phone against his ear, he wiped down the countertops. Her voicemail came on and he left her a message.

As he ended the call, he heard the name Océano on the radio and turned up the volume.

"So the man was rescued by a couple of residents, but he has no idea who he is. According to police sources, Océano, as he is being called, has an English accent and he has been hanging out at the Old Town section of Ibiza. Or as we all call it here, Eivissa." The announcer let a string of S's sound as he said the name.

"And you know . . . it's interesting, but I've learned that amnesia, or a fugue state, is more common in men than it is in women. Some men can walk around in that state for years."

"That explains your behavior then," a woman cracked. They both laughed.

Demetrio turned off the radio, walked outside, and looked for the local paper that was delivered daily. As usual it was lying on the small patch of grass that was automatically watered every night. The paper was soaking wet. He brought it inside to dry, poured himself a fresh cup of coffee, then picked up his cell phone, calling Stefano.

"How's our friend doing?" he asked when Stefan picked up on the third ring.

"There's a lot of reporters at the hospital. Somebody recognized Océano from the Internet. He's definitely English, but nobody's saying much. The police are here interviewing him. The doctors are bandaging his feet. I'll call you with any news I get."

"Thanks."

Feeling restless, Demetrio put a call in to one of his buddies who worked for the beach patrol council, asking about how he could go about erecting a memorial for Allister. They tossed around ideas, agreeing that a tree and a bench beside it with a small bronze plaque on it was a beautiful option.

"As long as the council doesn't have to pay for this memorial and you can keep it looking nice, I'll bring it up at our meeting on the third of next month," he said.

Demetrio counted out the fistful of money Stefano and Chenche had given him. He matched their sum and put the money in one of the plastic envelopes he used for his banking. He hid it under a bunch of towels in the linen closet.

Yawning, despite the coffee, he went back to bed, setting his clock for two hours. He'd nap a little longer, go back to the club, and handle his banking chores.

He sighed as he hit the sheets. Maybe he should have another cup of coffee and get on with his day. He'd hardly closed his eyes when he felt a warm hand on his thigh. His eyes flew open and the alarm rang. *My God. Who's in bed with me?* He turned to find Océano grinning at him.

"Time to wake up," Océano joked. Demetrio reached over and turned off the alarm. Océano was naked in bed with him, his hand now moving around Demetrio's belly for his cock.

"Yeah, I knew you were hard all night. You wanted me to fuck you, didn't you?"

Demetrio swallowed. Man, it was hard to dispute with his cock doing the happy dance in the guy's hand.

Océano stared at him, sliding closer to him in the bed.

"You're gay?" Demetrio whispered.

Océano shrugged. "I don't know. I do know that I got hit on by a bunch of chicks . . . and some men, but all I could think about was getting back into this bed and fucking the hell out of you, about how nice it would be to look down and see my cock right inside your fine ass."

Demetrio swallowed hard again. His cock was leaking against the man's searching fingers.

"I want to fuck you and make you come so hard," Océano said. "Will you let me?"

"Yes." *Fuck yes.*

He felt it now, Océano's determined cock pressing against his tailbone.

"We need rubbers."

"I know." Océano's grin widened. "They gave me some at the hospital. They also gave me some nice happy pills, bandaged my feet, and oh . . . I want to fuck you. I . . . know how to fuck but I . . . I'm not sure of what I'm doing here."

"You're not gay."

"I keep telling you I don't know. I do know I want you. God, your ass looks nice and tight." He gripped Demetrio's hip with on hand, balancing himself on his other elbow so that they lay side by side. He moved his hand from Demetrio's hip back to his leaking cock, using some of the lube on his fingers to rub against Demetrio's asshole.

God . . . clumsy yet so damned fucking hot!

Océano's breath grew shallow. He stopped speaking as his cock slid up and down Demetrio's crack. Demetrio loved the feel of a hot, hard cock against him. Océano's free hand moved back to Demetrio's cock. It sure was a nice way to get fucked. Demetrio loved taking it doggy style, but this way worked just as well.

He hugged Océano's cock between his ass cheeks and felt the rigid muscle pulsing against his skin. *God.*

Océano might think he didn't know what he was doing, but he had an orange foil square between his teeth now and even had the rubber out of the package and on his lips. Demetrio was surprised the hospital was giving out such exotic fare. The fruit-flavored rubbers were a special favorite of the gay crowd. Club Sugar gave them out freely to their customers.

Stefan. He must have given the rubbers to the hospital as part of a promotion. He's always coming up with creative ways to get his brand out there.

Océano rolled the rubber onto his cock. It was so sheer that when Demetrio glanced down over his shoulder at it, he had to look twice to make sure it was there.

"There's some lube on this," Océano said. "I'm not going

to hurt you, am I?"

"No."

Océano took his time, moving his hand lightly over Demetrio's cock and balls. He even reached over his shoulder and squeezed Demetrio's nipple.

Demetrio moaned. "Oh, I love that."

Océano kept his fingers there, rubbing the hardening bud as his cock sought entry into Demetrio, who raised one leg to give him easier access. It had been a few months since he'd been fucked, and it surprised him how much he wanted it, considering the guy hadn't kissed him. There was still some amazing raw passion here.

"God," Océano said as he entered Demetrio slowly. "I fucking knew it would feel like this." He moved more of himself into Demetrio until he was fully immersed. There was a moment where they grinned at one another as they both had what they wanted.

Full contact.

Océano began fucking him. He had a beautiful style, his movements assured and sensual. He swooped his hand down to Demetrio's yearning cock, claiming tenure of it again, moving his fingers up and down in a gentle yet determined rhythm.

He reached down, dropping kisses on Demetrio's shoulder and chin. He was clearly in orbit, his fucking increasing in tempo, bringing his mouth down again and again. Demetrio reached his arm up and around Océano so their mouths came into contact. It seemed to surprise Océano, who didn't pull away but began licking Demetrio's chin and throat. He moved his head down and around to Demetrio's chest, clamping his lips and tongue down on Demetrio's nipple.

"Fuck!" Demetrio shouted as he felt Océano's cock erupting inside him. Even with the rubber he could feel the man's relentless, heated twitching. He came just as hard, with

Océano's hand holding tightly onto his shaft.

Demetrio's thoughts turned to the absurd. *I bet he plays a beautiful game of tennis.*

Océano stayed in him for long minutes, his cock remaining hard. When he finally pulled out, they lay side by side for a moment.

"I guess I should tell you who I am," Océano said. "My name is Philip Gordon, and they say I'm a jewel thief."

CHAPTER FOUR

Whatever he'd been expecting, it wasn't that. Demetrio's postcoital high hadn't abated even though he heard the words "jewel thief." He'd also heard "they say I'm a jewel thief."

"You *are* a jewel thief, or they are saying you are?"

"I'm apparently a diamond appraiser, though I must say I'm surprised. I have no interest in diamonds. I couldn't tell you the first thing about them. I'm beginning to think they have to be wrong. I think the only reason the cops haven't arrested me is that there is no proof I stole anything. And I survived a systematic beating. They tell me my partner was murdered."

He stared up at the ceiling.

Demetrio said nothing as he raised himself on one elbow to look at Océano, or should he call him Philip? He was dismayed to see a tear trickle out of the corner of the man's eye.

"It's okay," he whispered, wiping away the tear with his index finger.

"I should have . . . I should have told you before we . . . you know . . ."

Demetrio shook his head. "It was still nice, and I don't believe you're a jewel thief."

A tremulous smile. Océano tilted his head toward him. "Will you still be my friend, or do you want me to go?"

"I want you to stay. But if it's jewels you're after, I don't have any."

Océano laughed, brushing the tears from his eyes. "Good

to know. I won't bother going through your drawers, then."

He sat up, took the rubber from his cock, tied off the end, and walked with it into the bathroom. He came right back out again. Damn, Oceano's dick was still half-hard. It was a shame he wanted to run off just as they were having fun, but on the other hand, the guy had just said he might possibly be a jewel thief.

"Do you have any plastic bags handy?" Océano asked. "I have to cover my feet. The bandages are not supposed to get wet."

"Yes, in the kitchen cupboard."

"Great, thanks." He gave Demetrio a quick smile and headed to the kitchen.

Demetrio lay for a few minutes, trying to absorb what he'd heard. The shower started running a minute later. He wanted to pee, but he wanted to leave the man alone to clean himself up in peace. Demetrio used the other bathroom instead, his mind rambling over the new developments.

Man, why did he have to be a bad guy? The next thing he thought was, *I don't think he is. I just don't buy it.*

He slipped back into bed again, feeling chilly. When Océano came back into the room, Demetrio realized he'd been dozing again.

"Hey," he said when Océano came and sat on the edge of the bed. "What should I call you?"

"Can you please call me Océano?"

"Of course."

"I took my shower with the plastic bags. That's the closest I'm gonna get to the ocean for a couple of days. Besides, I like Océano."

"Good, because you know what's weird, you don't look like a Philip Gordon."

Océano's expression turned grave. "Listen, I'm starting to remember some things, and I think I'm in trouble. I can't say much, but I need to make a few calls. I promise you're in no danger, but I need to borrow your cell phone. Is that okay?"

"Is this about your partner?"

"Yes." He blew out a sigh. "It's my fault he's dead. I need to deal with this, and I don't have much time."

"What does that mean? Are they about to arrest you?"

He shook his head. "I can't say right now. When the time is right, I will. I promise. Is it okay if I make some calls?"

"Go right ahead." Demetrio reached over and handed the guy some fresh clothes.

"We should shop for runners for you."

Océano's cheeks flushed. "Stefan and Chenche bought me some. They've been very kind. You all have. I left the shoes in the kitchen, but, um, can I borrow some socks?"

Demetrio smiled and opened the drawer. "Help yourself."

Océano picked out a pair and left the room. When he was gone, Demetrio stepped into the bathroom and took his own shower. He saw the spent rubber lying in the wastebasket. *That was a fun fuck. Man, it was hot!*

Taking a quick shower, he got dressed and found his recent bed buddy in the kitchen, pacing as he spoke on the phone. His stress was acute and it saddened Demetrio to see it. Somehow, he had a strong conviction the man was no crook. He went to the closet and retrieved his plastic envelope.

"I have to go back to the club," he said when he caught Océano's gaze.

Océano nodded, ended his call, and handed the phone back to him.

"Stefan said he'd help me get a cell phone today. I'll come back to the club with you."

They fell into step. Océano seemed distracted and worried. "Is there anything I can do to help you?" Demetrio asked.

Océano shook his head. "Not right now. Do you have to work tonight?"

"For a while. Why?"

"I thought it might be nice to have dinner with you."

That surprised him, but then, Océano was full of surprises lately.

"I'd like that, thank you."

"Okay, cool." They'd arrived at Santa Lucia Street, which was just starting to come to life.

"Will you be here most of the afternoon?" Océano asked.

"No, I have some banking to do, and then I thought I'd take a walk up in the forest."

Océano gaped at him. "There's a forest here?"

Demetrio laughed. "A beautiful forest."

"I'd like to go with you."

"But . . . your feet."

"I'm on happy pills, remember? And now they're band-aged, they feel great. I'd like to see your forest. How about we meet in two hours back here at Club Dino? I have to go meet with Stefan, and I still have some more calls to make."

Before Demetrio could respond, Océano stepped forward and kissed him. It was a sweet, short kiss, but nonetheless a thrilling surprise. Océano walked across the road as a golf cart with three surfboards stacked on the canvas roof careened past them at a dangerous tilt.

Demetrio recognized the guys as locals and waved to them when they shouted out his name. He caught Océano's scowl as he reached the other side of the road.

"And no flirting!" Océano called out, making him smile.

He watched the golf cart wobbling its way down to the ocean. In summer nobody would be able to ride a cart or a bike of any kind. This area would be filled shoulder to shoulder with people walking, day and night.

Inside the bar, Jeanine, looking like a twinkly canary in an outfit encrusted with yellow sequins, accosted him from her perch on a stool. She was drinking a nine-lives cocktail, a lethal mix of three different rums and pineapple juice. She always matched her drinks with her outfits.

"He's a jewel thief."

"Oh, shut up."

"Well, if you can't handle reality —"

"Jeanine, please keep your mouth shut until you know what you are talking about."

"I heard it on the news."

Great, just great.

"They think he's —"

"Yes, I know. They *think*. Until we know for sure . . . until an arrest is made and we're in possession of all the facts, let's not gossip about the man, shall we?"

"Oh fuck. You bonked him."

It was a statement, not a question, and anyway it was none of her damned business. He saw the hurt look in her eyes. "Sorry. I just think we need to get all the facts."

She gave him a sympathetic smile. "If you ever need to talk, I'll be the one grateful for not being behind the bar polishing the glasses." Jeanine gave him a little pat on the shoulder.

Was she being sarcastic about the fact he'd blocked her from working the bar this weekend? He didn't think so. Wait. She was being nice. *Oh. I'm the object of pity.* Demetrio closed his eyes. Now *he* was on the receiving end of relationship advice.

Demetrio moved away as she took her seat again, and a slightly drunk young man stepped in front of him. "Your female bartender."

"Er, yes?" Demetrio couldn't tell from the man's glassy gaze if he was about to hear good news or bad news.

"She gave me a massage."

Oh, God. Demetrio waited for the punch line and the man said, "Yeah. I went to that salon where she works. I got a great massage and somehow wound up going home with two kittens, but I didn't get her number." His face flushed. It was cute, actually. "You think she's single? Would she date me?"

"Why don't you ask her?" Demetrio suggested.

"Is she single?" the guy asked again.

"Yes, she's single."

"She's so pretty. How could she be?"

"Jeanine works all the time," Demetrio said. "She juggles three jobs, plus the cat rescues. I've no idea how she does it." It was the truth and he could see now that she was leaning over the bar laughing with the shirtless guys pouring drinks. "Come on, I'll buy you a cocktail." Demetrio tugged the guy along with him and leaned past the human crush to talk to Jeanine, who as usual smelled of something flowery and beguiling. "Get whatever drinks you want. They're on me."

"Thanks, boss." Jeanine and her client grinned at each other. Demetrio hoped it was the start of something beautiful for them. His cell phone rang. *Unknown Call.* He answered anyway, half-expecting it to be some idiotic telemarketing goofball wanting to sell him penile enlargement equipment. He'd never worried about his size before, but the influx of these calls and the follow-up emails and text messages sometimes made him wonder.

He thought about Océano's nice big cock and was surprised to hear the man's deep voice.

"Ha! I memorized your number correctly. Listen, pick any restaurant you want to go to for dinner tonight, okay?"

Demetrio grinned. "Am I paying?"

"Yes, sweetheart, you are." A chuckle. "But I'll make it up to you."

Demetrio laughed too. "Oh? How do you plan to do that?"

"Now that would be telling, wouldn't it? Are you going to the bank now?"

"Soon."

"Okay. Wait for me. I want to go with you."

"You don't need to."

"I want to."

"That would be nice."

They ended the call, Demetrio's head spinning. What the hell is wrong with me? I'm acting like I haven't had a date in months. Well, I haven't really. Not anyone I want to see a second time . . .

Océano was like a little kid accompanying him to the bank. Barclay's, the British bank, had branches in a few of the Balearic Islands, and their English, of course, was very good. Demetrio had some trouble opening his account initially, but Stefan had helped him, giving him useful tips such as registering himself as a resident within days of his arrival to expedite the efficiency of his checking account. He'd opened it in euros, which played havoc initially since British banks still worked with pounds sterling. Now he was an official resident, the bank had stopped trying to charge him extra fees for currency conversion.

He'd discovered it was one of the many quirks of the financial life of people in Eivissa. He finished making his deposit and pocketed the slips.

"Why did you make two deposits to the same account?" Océano asked.

"One payment is for a memorial we're organizing for a former resident."

"That's nice of you. Was he a close friend?"

"Not really, but I liked him."

"Was he your lover?"

"No. Never."

As they walked out of the bank, they encountered Stefan and Chenche. Chenche looked cranky.

He instantly perked up. "My friends are here!" He rushed over, hugging and kissing Demetrio and Océano. "My husband wants to bank. Always with the bank."

Stefan rolled his eyes. "Can you hang out with the drama queen? I need to pop inside for a moment."

Demetrio grinned.

"Where are you going now?" Chenche asked, cuddling Demetrio for a moment before turning his affection toward Océano.

"A walk in the hills."

"Beautiful! Me, too!"

Demetrio doubted it. Chenche wore nothing but stark white shorts that, while slightly baggy, hung low on his hips, low enough to reveal a delicious treasure trail disappearing into the crotch line.

When Stefan returned, Chenche threw himself at him. "Let's go for a walk!"

Stefan kissed him. "Okay!"

He pointed to his car. "We have the car. We actually had planned to go up to the mountain."

"See, I told you," Chenche said, throwing his arms around Demetrio. They climbed into the car, Chenche in front with Stefan.

"It's such a beautiful island." Océano seemed awed by the stunning view as they climbed higher and higher. They entered the old town of Sant Josep and joined the jumble of cars parked against the side of the road.

"There's a wonderful trail the old lumberjacks and coal miners used to take to the mountain here," Stefan told Océano. "The mountain, *Sa Taila*, is beautiful."

"How long is the walk?"

"About two hours, but it isn't difficult. Maybe we can start, and you can see how you feel."

"I'd like that."

A few serious backpackers brushed past them, but Demetrio and his friends took things a little slower. As they started walking, Chenche was in a frolicsome mood and let them pass. He plucked at Demetrio's hand. "Why won't you make love with me?"

"Ah, Chenche, what can I say? If anything ever happens to your husband, I need a whole weekend with you. One night won't be enough."

Chenche laughed. "Then I will push him off a cliff right now!"

"Hey," Océano said, separating them. "Cut that out. He's mine now."

"Yours?" Chenche looked surprised.

"Yes." Océano put his arm around Demetrio. "Now show me everything about your wonderful trail."

Chenche reached for the top button of his shorts.

"Not that trail." Océano laughed.

Chenche feigned a pout and skipped ahead like a little kid, grabbing his husband's hand. They danced and jumped, hands swinging between them. Demetrio started pointing out places of interest, which was difficult with Océano's mouth suddenly on his.

"I'm beset by the urge to kiss you and fuck you all night long."

Demetrio shook his head. "Now he tells me."

Ahead of them, they could see Chenche's head.

"He's still skipping," Océano observed. "He's so goofy, it's hard for me to be mad at him, even though he keeps making passes at you."

"Oh, he makes passes at everybody."

"As long as you don't take him up on it."

Océano kissed him again, grabbed his hand, and they ran to join the others. They passed several old rural houses. Demetrio found himself gazing at them longingly. He loved these mountains and the ten sixteenth-century towers often called the Pirate Towers. From here, islanders once kept watch for pirates and other possible attacks from foreign ships that streamed in from Turkey and the Barbary Coast. Those days were long gone. What remained was a sense of timeless peace. Sometimes he fantasized about renting out a house here and getting away from it all, from the tiny streets and nonstop people.

"What's the matter?" Océano pressed his hand.

"Nothing. I just love these houses."

"It's amazing up here. I can smell pine trees. The view is breathtaking. It's like a fairy paradise."

"I know." Demetrio sighed. "I'd love to spend the winter months up here."

"Why don't you?"

Demetrio shrugged. "Maybe I will, now that I think about it."

The problem was Demetrio had come here to fight his inclination to hibernate and isolate. And yet, if he were to give in to his inner hermit crab, he would be very happy up here and wouldn't need company. So why did he keep visualizing himself here with Océano?

Because he's the first guy I've liked in a long, long time.

They passed a tiny church, its bells ringing merrily. They passed aromatic fig trees and deep green vines to walk inside, taking in the beautiful, rough-hewn altarpiece made of wood and stone. Through the few open stained-glass windows, the smell of pine, fennel, and, he noted, pungent rosemary could be detected. Like the towers, the church had been built with pirate attacks in mind with high stone windows and ledges, large enough to accommodate a man and a weapon. Demetrio had learned that in ancient times, two men always manned the stone towers, sending smoke signals in times of distress. Those days seemed so far away now with nothing but the swaying of leaves in the sunshine and the swinging church bell in the slight breeze creating a hypnotic sense of peace. Chenche gazed lovingly at a gold icon of the baby Jesus and led the others in a giddy round of stuffing the donation box by the door with some euros. They passed outside again, the air invigorating and fresh.

Demetrio could never get used to how picturesque Eivissa was. He heard the soft snorting of horses and the rhythmic clopping of hooves as a couple of riders passed them. They all exchanged greetings. Demetrio felt woozy with the sense of timelessness. He wanted to absorb it all and wear it close like a second skin.

"This," Chenche said, waving his arms around, "is *my* church. This fills my soul."

They had dinner that night at the Golden Buddha, one of Demetrio's favorite restaurants on the island. As the name implied, there was a golden Buddha out front, and in spite of being right on the beach, it had somehow remained a mostly locals-only establishment, with most people speaking in Spanish.

Stefan and Chenche had insisted on joining them. After opening his bar and leaving his staff to handle things, Demetrio had suggested the Golden Buddha, and it was clear as he sipped an apple martini that Océano loved it here. As the sun set, infusing the place with a soft, golden glow, he turned to Demetrio.

"I want to remember this moment. No matter what I remember in the future about my past, this is one moment I will never forget, being here with you."

Demetrio was overcome by those words. He caught Stefan's sweet smile and Chenche's discrete thumbs-up. One day, if he needed a reminder that Océano had said these things, he was glad he had witnesses.

Océano's hand moved to Demetrio's lap. "Now, sweetheart, what do you recommend?"

"I'll order," Demetrio said. "I know the chef, and I already called him, and he told me the fish that have just been caught."

Chenche gazed at Stefan adoringly. It wasn't a look one

saw very often, but Demetrio knew that in spite of everything, all the crazy sex games, the men, and the mad movies, Chenche loved his man very, very much.

"We have to come here often," Océano said when their appetizers of grilled scorpion fish arrived. "How wonderfully unexpected. Who would have known that such a scary-looking fish with poisonous spikes could be so sweet and juicy. I've never tasted anything like this," he said of the garlic- and lemon-infused Balearic specialty. He licked his fork. "I love this place."

Their meal was fun, with each of them sampling one another's dishes. Demetrio had always eaten family style with Stefan and Chenche, and though he detected a moment of resistance from Océano, he too, happily shared the dishes put in front of him, except his dessert of baked Alaska.

"Sorry," he said, putting his arm around his still-flaming dish, "this is all mine!"

Demetrio tried to pay the check, but Stefan had beaten him to it, apparently handing their waiter his credit card as soon as they arrived.

"We pay next time," Demetrio insisted.

Océano reached for his knee under the table and squeezed.

Afterward when Stefan returned his car to its parking space in a garage around the corner from where he and Chenche lived, they all walked back to their little neighborhood.

Océano had fielded the odd gentle question from the other three over his real identity, but now, he admitted, Philip Gordon wasn't his real name.

"It's all I can tell you," he said.

"Oh, I love mysteries!" Chenche clapped his hands together. "I know you're no jewel thief. Why do they think you are?"

"You don't think I am?"

"No. I just don't feel it."

"I don't either," Demetrio said, relieved he had backup on this point.

Océano seemed pleased. "Good. That's all I can say for now."

"So we still call you Océano?" Stefan's smile was playful.

"Yes, please. I am Océano, and now I want to go dancing!"

"Me too!" Chenche said.

Demetrio wanted to check in with his work crew and was pleased when they all walked in and found the two Spanish guitarists more or less sober and the place was hopping.

"I need noise! I need something loud!" Chenche shouted, dashing across the road with Stefan.

"Come on," Océano urged, grabbing Demetrio's hand. "Let's have fun."

Boy, he was one surprise after another.

They ran over to Sugar, where Chenche was already dancing with some of his clubbers. Stefan was behind the bar mixing drinks, cell phone glued to his ear.

Océano shocked Demetrio by wanting to dance Eivissa style. "Take your T-shirt off," he shouted in Demetrio's ear.

"Are you stoned or something?"

Océano made a tsking sound. "Don't you want to dance with me?"

"Yes . . . but you hate this music and . . . and . . . what about your feet?"

"They're fine. I'm not climbing anymore mountains today, but I survived those, didn't I? Now take off the fucking T-shirt."

Demetrio did as he was told. Océano removed his shirt too, and they let them trail from the back of their pants as Océano took him in his arms and they moved to the music. Their cocks began grinding against one another, Océano cupping Demetrio's ass cheeks, pulling him closer. Demetrio again felt that wonderful sense of drowning in timeless bliss, but this was a different emotion. What he felt for Océano was pure and raw and took his breath away. It was quick fire. It was insanity and it was very, very beautiful.

When Océano kissed him, the musical beat slowed and the two of them began kissing in earnest.

"Come with me," Demetrio shouted, breaking off their kiss. He thought they were both in danger of coming in their pants. He had something much better in mind. He took Océano's hand and led him to one of the upstairs rooms. As they squeezed past the throng of hot, hard bodies in motion, Demetrio caught a glimpse of Stefan and Chenche up against a wall.

Stefan's pants hung loosely on his muscular thighs, Chenche's legs wrapped around his waist. They were obviously fucking, but they were lost to everyone else. Demetrio looked in every tiny alcove and dark corner until he found a tiny chaise in a darkened room overlooking the ocean.

"Sit," he commanded. Océano sat, Demetrio kneeling between his legs. He fumbled with the zipper on Océano's pants and was thrilled when Océano's underpants emerged with a big wet spot right where his cockhead lay wedged.

"Oh man." Océano's ass came off the small chaise, and Demetrio pulled down the pants and briefs, shooting his tongue out at the cock waving in his face.

Océano watched him, Demetrio could feel it, but he closed his eyes, savoring every second of blowing the man. He wanted this to be an incredible experience. Holding Océano's cock in both hands, he rubbed it in his palms. He'd dated a tantric expert for a few months, and the guy had taught him some nifty tricks. He let the cock harden between his palms and fingers before beginning a rolling motion he knew from practicing on himself would start causing a wonderful tight sensation in Océano's balls. He heard Océano moan, and began letting the cockhead slap against his tongue as he rolled the man's cock back and forth in his hands.

"Oh, oh . . . suck it, for God's sake, suck me!"

Demetrio did just that, sucking on Océano, enjoying the tangy taste of the other man's pre-come in his mouth. Océano fucked his mouth with increasingly eager strokes. Demetrio didn't pull back. He worked on relaxing his throat muscles, taking the entire shaft into his mouth. Océano was beyond excited now. His cockhead seemed to mushroom. His hands came up and rested lightly on Demetrio's head, but he didn't force him to suck.

He came hard, shooting deep into Demetrio's throat. Demetrio practiced every deep-breathing exercise he knew so he wouldn't gag on the monster cock in this throat.

When he eventually released Océano, he put a couple of kisses on the leaking cockhead and gazed up at him and smiled.

Océano looked dazed as he leaned back, staring down at him.

"I'll tell you one thing," Océano said, his voice hoarse. "No woman ever sucked my cock like that. I'd remember it. You just fucking amaze me."

They ran back over to the small room above Club Dino. Océano wanted to be back inside Demetrio, and Demetrio was happy to comply. They fucked like demented bunnies as the party raged downstairs. For hours Océano drilled him, and Demetrio had never enjoyed himself more. When they collapsed in a sated, sweaty heap a little after two in the morning, Demetrio found he was smiling. Océano fell asleep, his hair in wet tendrils as his head lay on Demetrio's shoulder.

Borrowed time. Why that thought struck Demetrio right then, he wasn't sure, but he looked at the time on his cell phone, and with a sigh, extricated himself from his new lover.

"Where are you going?" Océano's head came off his

shoulder.

"I need to go downstairs and make sure we close up on time."

"Want me to come?"

Demetrio shook his head. "Get some rest. I'm sure your feet would be happy for it."

"Yeah . . . they are starting to ache. I should take some happy pills."

"Yes, or get more . . ." Océano's eyes drifted closed as Demetrio finished his sentence," . . . sleep."

He got up and grabbed his clothes. After checking up and down the hall, he darted into the loo opposite and cleaned himself up before heading downstairs. The party still seemed in full swing.

"We had a small problem about an hour ago," one of his bartenders told him.

"Problem?"

Charlie, one of his best, most efficient employees, had worked the clubs in Eivissa for years. A British expat, he adored the island, and in the off-season returned to mainland Spain, where he continued his work in several clubs as a DJ and a bartender. In his late thirties, he was handsome in a hardened way. He'd worked as a bouncer in England, tried his hand at a little gay porn, and after three movies, vanished into the club scene.

He handed Demetrio a credit card. "We had a customer who used it for one round of drinks and told us to keep an open tab."

Demetrio nodded. It was the custom, and only rarely did they have a problem. When it did arise, the matter was usually handled with cash and there were no hard feelings.

"It's stolen. We couldn't run it a second time. We called the hotline. They told us to hold the guy until the police arrived. They had let the first charge through, thinking they had a lead on him. He's been using this card all over the islands. He's been to Minorca, Majorca . . . and now he's here."

"He got away?"

The bartender nodded. "As soon as he saw me on the phone, he gave his pals the signal and they fled."

"How much are we out?"

"Five hundred."

It was a bad loss. Five hundred euros was around four hundred British pounds or seven hundred US dollars. Demetrio always converted euros in his mind since he was still getting used to dealing with them on a daily basis.

He looked at the tab Charlie handed him. The men who'd tried passing the credit card had bought several hefty rounds of drinks and a bottle of Cristal champagne.

"The champagne was the last thing they ordered?"

"Yes. And it was expensive, the Louis Roederer two thousand and two. So of course I ran the card just to be sure, and bam! It's a hot deal."

"Thank you for running the card when you did."

"I wish we'd gotten word it was a hot card before they got the bottle. They left it, but unfortunately it was already open."

Demetrio realized one of the new bartenders must have given them the bottle, and Charlie thought to check the card.

"I hope you all had some."

"We did, and it's fantastic. If I'm ever stupid enough to steal a credit card, the Louis is the first thing I'm gonna buy."

Demetrio laughed. The situation was unfortunate, but he was lucky he had good bartenders who followed all the rules. No club owner liked being ripped off. Demetrio looked at the card and balked. The name on it was Philip Gordon. It couldn't have been a coincidence. It was a Barclay's credit card.

"What are we supposed to do with the card?"

"Keep it. The police are coming for it as soon as we close

the club. They want to talk to you. You notice the name on it?"

Demetrio nodded. So it wasn't lost on Charlie either. He thought about going upstairs and waking up Océano, but to what end? They'd discuss it soon enough. Demetrio knew he could claim the loss on taxes, but still, it bugged him. What the hell kind of crap had Océano gotten himself into?

"People have been asking about him all night," Charlie said. "All kinds of rumors are flying around."

"Really."

It was a statement that didn't invite further response. Charlie was smart enough to drop the subject, and Demetrio moved behind the bar to help handle the crush of last drink requests.

When Océano drifted in around closing time, Demetrio bristled. He wanted to talk to the man before the cops arrived. He also had to get a few recalcitrant stragglers out of the club.

"What's wrong?" Océano asked, obviously sensing Demetrio's distress.

"We got a credit card with your name on it. The cops will be here soon. We need to talk."

Océano opened his mouth, but Demetrio had to eject the revelers before the cops started showing up and adding fines to all his other current woes. Océano stepped in and helped him.

"Thanks, guys," Demetrio told his staff. "You can all go home now."

"Want me to stay, boss?" Charlie asked.

Demetrio hesitated. Of course, Charlie had to stay. Demetrio rubbed his temples. He felt like he was losing his mind. He had to start thinking straight. Charlie had seen the perpetrator and could identify him.

"Who was the bartender serving the customer?" he asked.

Charlie grimaced. "Jeanine."

"Jeanine? But I told her she couldn't work this weekend."

Demetrio also thought she might fall for her massage client. *Oh God. She's gone and fallen for a criminal instead.*

Charlie shrugged. "She was hanging out in the club and just took one look at the customer and got behind the bar and took over." He shot Demetrio a look of rebuke. "You weren't here, and we were busy. I tried to keep my eye on her, but it was nuts. When I saw the frickin' champagne heading their way, I stepped in and swiped the credit card."

"Champagne?" Océano seemed to pale.

"Cristal," Charlie told him.

"I want you to stay," Demetrio said. When the others had gone and only Charlie remained, Demetrio turned to him. "I want you to tell Océano what happened here tonight."

Charlie launched into his story.

"Where is Jeanine now?" Demetrio asked.

"She took off with the customer and his companions. I tried to stop her. She just wouldn't listen."

"Oh my God. Should we report her missing?"

"Don't panic yet," Océano said. "Maybe she just followed them, and they blew her off." He turned to Charlie. "What did this customer look like?"

Charlie considered the question. "Good-looking blond guy. I mean, I'd take him home and fuck him. Kind of a young Robert Redford but without the bad skin. He was well-dressed." Charlie suddenly grinned. "He was wearing an outfit I saw in the window of Luis Moneo only this morning. A pretty nifty Moschino."

Luis Moneo was one of the few menswear-only stores on the island. You could certainly find deals there in the off-season, but everything in the store now would be current and the latest, hottest trends in Europe.

"You think he used the credit card there?" Océano asked.

Charlie gave him an appreciative glance. "The credit card company said he'd hit Eivissa this afternoon."

"It worries me that he came here," Océano mused.

"You think you know this guy?" Demetrio asked.

Océano glanced at him and back at Charlie. "Tell me, did this handsome, younger Robert Redford have a speech impediment? Did he stutter?"

Charlie looked surprised. "Yes, he did."

Océano didn't react. He merely pulled out his cell phone. "I have to make a call." He stepped away from them.

"What a clusterfuck," Charlie said. "Should we start cleaning up?"

"I guess. Have you cleaned up the glassware from the customer?"

"We held on to the glass he'd been using with the champagne. I thought about fingerprints. The credit card would be useless because so many of us touched it."

"Good thinking," Demetrio said, and began helping Charlie with the last of the bar cleanup.

When Océano returned, he was still on the phone. He asked for 'Philip Gordon's' tab again and checked it, muttering into his phone. We he ended his call, he started asking Charlie questions. Charlie answered them. He was a wise man, and like every damned good bartender, something of a counter therapist.

"Jesus Christ, you're a copper, aren't you?"

"Yes." Océano glanced at Demetrio, his gaze returning to Charlie. "And if the man you're describing is who I think he is, then you're all in danger the longer I stay here."

"Why? Who is he?" Demetrio demanded.

They all jumped when they heard a hard knock at the door.

"It's the police." Demetrio's legs inexplicably shook. He was having a hard time processing the news the man he'd had such wild, intoxicating sex with, was a cop.

I knew he wasn't a bad guy. I just knew it.

CHAPTER FIVE

Alférez Apolinar, Jaime to Demetrio, took possession of the credit card, the tab, and the champagne glass, impressed Charlie had thought to hold on to it. He told the bartender they would bring in photos for him to look at later in the day.

"We are waiting for photos from Madrid," Jaime said. There wasn't a lot of criminal activity on Eivissa, and he and the other officers seemed to be enjoying this little drama.

They glanced at Océano but seemed wary of him. When Demetrio mentioned Jeanine leaving with the suspect—as the police had referred to him—they took her details and said they'd look into it.

"We'll be in touch," they said, but their gazes were on Océano.

When Charlie finally left the club and it was just the two of them, Demetrio turned to him.

"Wanna explain?"

Océano winced. "No, I can't."

"Can't, or won't?" Demetrio was furious. "Jesus Christ, Océano. You've been in my home. You've been in my bed. For fuck's sake . . . you've been inside me. I deserve some respect here. A fucking stranger came in here and ripped me off!"

"Okay, okay . . . look, I never meant this to happen. I . . . I like you. We were having fun and this has been an incredible day. I just wish it could be more. I wish . . . I wish this island . . . I wish being with you was reality. But it's not. It's a beautiful fantasy. All I can tell you is this, because I don't re-member everything and . . . some of it is still privileged infor-mation."

Demetrio's back teeth ground against each other. *A beauti-ful fantasy. Shit.*

"I'm a British fraud detective. Scotland Yard. Over a year ago, I was assigned to an undercover operation spanning three countries. I've been posing as a big-time drug and weap-ons dealer. You probably know there are lots of terror cells infiltrating Italy and Spain, and we finally got a lead on one of the biggest."

Demetrio watched the guy swallow.

"Are you in pain?"

"Yeah." Océano nodded. He fished into his pocket for a couple of his happy pills. Demetrio poured him a glass of Per-rier. Océano's hands shook as he downed the pills. "Christ, my feet feel like they're on fire."

"Sit." Demetrio's natural instincts were to nurture. He put a couple of the chairs down at a table and forced Océano to take a seat. He found a basin under the sink, ran some warm water into it, and dropped some Epsom salts into the water. He stirred it and brought it over to Océano, who put his feet into it after Demetrio removed his socks, shoes, and very grimy bandages.

"That feels better." Océano kicked his feet in the warm wa-ter, relief flooding his face.

"I have a first-aid kit upstairs. I think there are bandages in it, but first I want to hear what you have to tell me."

Océano haltingly laid out his story. "Everything I'm about to say to you is in confidence, okay?"

"Okay."

"My partner, Joshua . . . we had a cover. We were brothers with too much money. We were authorized to make small purchases of arms and drugs. We got some attention because people realized we had money and we were willing to spend it. Long story short, the guy who came in here tonight . . . he was there when Joshua died. He was the ringleader."

Océano's eyes teared up. "It was a mistake. A horrible, bloody cock-up. We were set up. Somehow, they found out who we were. I keep remembering snatches of conversation. I know I got hit from behind on the back of the head. I remember saying, 'There must be some mistake,' but they knew. The bastards fucking *knew.*

"We thought the whole thing was laid out . . . we went to make a big purchase over in Majorca . . . we went in my boat . . . well, Philip Gordon's boat. We met them in a cave. There's a whole bunch of pirate caves. They're saying I shot Joshua, but I know it isn't possible."

"I don't understand. You went to meet them and Joshua winds up dead, you wind up getting beaten, and—"

"Yes! They thought I was dead. I remember lying on the ground. They kicked me a couple of times. I played dead. Jesus, that was hard. I had no idea if Joshua was alive or dead, but I guess I knew, deep down, I knew he was gone. When they picked his body up and tossed him deep into a cave, I knew I was next. Fuck . . . they buried him. I couldn't keep up the ruse and get buried alive. I crawled to my boat and I got into it. I think that's when I hurt my feet. I tumbled over the edge. I remember it was high. I still don't know how I got away. I hear the gunshot that killed him, you know. I hear it night and day. I hear Joshua begging for his life."

"And you didn't shoot him?"

"No. Of course I didn't. But you're going to hear a lot of crazy stories. I'm going to have to go on trial. They'll say I went deep undercover and that I started believing my own bullshit. It's total rubbish. Look, I wanted out. I wanted my fucking life back."

"How did they get your credit card?"

"As soon as I saw it tonight, it came back to me. When we

arrived at the meeting point, they stripped our money belts from us. I had a cell phone, a gun, some cash, and a couple of cards. Two were dummies, one was active. That's the card he was using here tonight. You know I have to leave soon, don't you?"

Demetrio was startled by the sudden question. He knew he should have started running a million miles away from this man. He should have strapped on his bionic bloody fins and started swimming to another island, another galaxy even, but his ragged emotions wouldn't let him.

"When?"

"I don't know yet. Maybe tomorrow."

Demetrio nodded. "What do you want to do now?" He was amazed at how calm and assured he sounded, even to himself.

"Go home and sleep with you and pretend this is my life, that I get to sleep with you every night. That we close this place at absurd hours and go home and fuck like lunatics, falling asleep when the rest of the world is just waking up."

Demetrio's heart seemed to squeeze a little. He wanted to tell the guy to fuck off, that he was no fantasy. This was no fantasy. What they had was wonderful. It could be real.

"Can you handle it?"

Demetrio sucked in a breath. "I wouldn't trade what we have for anything."

"Oh fuck, sweetheart, don't say that. We have . . . nothing. What we have is astonishing and, Christ, so painfully sweet, but it isn't real. I'm not gay. I can't be gay. I can't involve you in this madness. These are very bad men, and I have to keep you as far away from this as I can. But for tonight I want to dream. And I want to believe in beautiful impossibilities. I want to believe in Eivissa."

Demetrio absorbed the words, wanting to remember it all, to fight off the inevitable.

"Let me get you a towel and some fresh bandages."

As he rummaged upstairs for what he needed, thoughts collided in his brain. His backbone had just become a wishbone. He knew he should shut the door on Océano, but he couldn't. Just couldn't. Downstairs he sat in front of him, lifting Océano's feet onto his lap, drying them and rebandaging them. He tried to assemble his thoughts.

"You . . . were you ever involved with Joshua?"

"Fuck. What a question. No. But . . . since you ask, I loved him. I still don't know what kind of love. I'm still struggling with losing him, with losing all the momentum we gained in this operation. He wanted it to happen, and we talked about it a couple of times. You get very close to a man when you're living in such . . . difficult circumstances. He felt we had to give it a chance, but he usually said this after a few glasses of wine. But yes, there were feelings there."

"But you believe you're straight."

"Oh no, I *am* straight. I have a ton of hot women in my past who will verify that."

"So . . . where do I fit into the sexual scheme of things?"

"You're my ultimate fantasy."

Demetrio said nothing. This poor guy was sadly deluded. He was, at the least, deeply bisexual, but right now Océano had more on his plate than his sexual identity to deal with. He put Océano's socks and shoes back on his feet.

"They feel fantastic. You did a better job than the nurse did at the hospital." He leaned over and kissed him. "Thank you."

They walked home together and showered, Demetrio not hesitating to soap the guy down with his best and most favorite Dolce & Gabbana body shampoo.

"I like the smell," Océano said, his head tilted back as Demetrio ran his hands over Océano's body. "It makes me think of freshly mowed grass."

"That's what it is. I'd love for you to fuck me on freshly cut grass."

Océano's head snapped back and his eyes gleamed. "If there's time before I leave, I will."

He took the sponge from Demetrio's hands, and as steam swirled around them, he soaped Demetrio's front and started working on his shoulders.

"Turn around, Demetrio."

He did as he was told. Océano started working on his back as the water ran in warm, wonderful rivulets to his ass. That wasn't the only thing that went there. He was stunned when Océano's fingers moved to his ass crack and he began soaping Demetrio with gentle squeezes of the sponge. When his warm breath hit Demetrio's asshole, he held his breath.

Océano's tongue flickered, timidly at first, then with increasing pressure against him. "Fuck. I gotta fuck you."

Demetrio remained where he was and heard his lover getting out of the tub.

"There are some rubbers in the medicine cabinet," he said.

He heard the mirrored door open and close, heard the tearing of a foil package, and held his breath again as Océano got back into the tub, crouched behind him, and resumed sucking and licking his ass.

When he finally stood, the water started turning cool, but Demetrio didn't care. He planted his feet apart, keeping his hands on the tiled wall for support, and stuck his ass out to Océano, who gripped his hips and began poking his rigid cock at Demetrio's waiting ass. With all the fucking they'd been doing, there was a small moment of sharp pain followed by an incredible feeling of peace. He'd never loved being fucked so much. In his life he normally topped, but this was something else. He gave himself up to the pleasure, delighting at the way Océano took hold of Demetrio's cock and began stroking it, taking pride in making him come as well. He heard his lover's balls slap against his ass and felt the slight pressure of them as Océano fucked him vigorously.

They came together hard, Demetrio's grip on the wall loosening. He almost fell and found himself bent over, Océano letting out a cry as he got deeper access to Demetrio.

When it was over, they turned off the taps and dried one another, returning to the bed hand in hand, their cocks hard.

"Sorry to tell you," Demetrio whispered as they reached for one another in the bed, "but I think you might just be a little bit gay."

"Shut up," Océano said, but he had a smile on his face.

Demetrio scooted down to lick and suck the man's balls and cock, moving to his ass.

"Oh my God, I never had a woman do this to me." Océano's legs flew open as Demetrio made a determined path to his asshole. "Don't think you can fuck me," he said.

"Don't worry, I won't." Demetrio settled for stroking the man's ass as he finally took possession of Océano's cock with his mouth, bringing him to another rousing climax.

"Damn," Océano said. "Fucking hot damn."

They fell asleep in one another's arms. When Demetrio awoke in the morning, he was surprised to see Océano lying beside him, his hand on Demetrio's cock.

"I think you might be right," Océano said. "I might be a little bit gay. I can't do this, though, D. You are so good, so kind and so fucking hot . . . but I have to go. I *have* to go."

"Christ. When?"

"Now." His voice came out hoarsely as he let go of Demetrio's cock. He had said he'd be leaving, but Demetrio wasn't ready. But then again, he never would be ready.

"Where are you going to go?"

"I don't know. I have to go back to England. They're sending someone to get me . . . But I feel I have to leave you. I can't keep doing this. I don't want to confuse you."

Christ . . . . Demetrio remembered what it was like dealing with guys in his past who were just coming out. They often had zigzagging emotions, and usually the morning after brought on tons of guilt, shame, and mindless angst.

"You don't have to leave, you daft bugger. We'll just knock off the sex. How about I buy you breakfast, and we just hang out?"

Océano sat back on his heels on the bed and stared at him. "You . . . don't mind?"

"No, I don't mind."

"I like you, Demetrio. I'd love to hang out."

They showered together again, only this time they didn't fuck. Demetrio wondered whether Océano would want to fuck him later in the day and knew that he himself had to draw a line. They soaped each other's backs and butts and finally coaxed each other out of the shower and dried off. Once they'd dressed, they left the house and wandered up the street.

"I get breakfast foods delivered," he told Océano. "We can eat at the club."

"Cool."

They found the usual basket of baked goods waiting at the back door. Demetrio walked in, wondering if he should call Jeanine and check on her. He knew she could be prickly if he called her too early in the morning, but damn it, he was worried about her. He called and left her a voice mail message and also texted her. He called the police, leaving a message for one of the officers who'd come to the club earlier that morning.

As he brewed coffee, Océano opened the basket, admiring the contents. "You get this yummy stuff every day?" he asked, incredulous.

Yes, and it could be yours too. Demetrio simply smiled and poured out coffee. There was a knock at the back door.

Demetrio opened it, pleased to find Chenche and Stefan

there. They came in with armfuls of fresh oranges and pink grapefruit they'd picked from somebody's garden.

"My hubby likes to pinch fruit. He thinks it tastes better if you nick it from somebody else's tree," Stefan told Océano, who laughed.

"Your secret is safe with me."

Chenche grinned. "Forbidden fruit is sweetest, *querido*. Everybody knows that."

Stefan laughed. "Of course it is. Very sweet."

They turned on some music and sliced up the fruit, piling everything onto plates. They ate breakfast on the terrace. The two men got caught up on the little Océano was willing to tell them. Demetrio was surprised he told them quite a lot.

"I'm trusting you two. I have to leave soon, and I want you to look after Demetrio for me. Don't let some wolf break his heart, okay?"

Chenche's gaze seared right into Demetrio's heart. The look of pity almost killed him.

"We'll look after him," Stefan said, "until you come back."

Océano looked like he was going to protest, but then Chenche asked a question that seemed to derail him.

"Are you ever going to tell us your real name?"

"One day, but not now." He looked flustered when he glanced at Demetrio. "We got any more coffee, sweetheart?"

Demetrio's heart gave a lurch. Damn . . . he could get used to being this guy's sweetheart. After a second pot, they debated what to do next and ended up racing down to the beach to skinny dip. Océano was fun and certainly enjoyed grabbing Demetrio's cock every time a wave came.

"It's our favorite game," Stefan told him.

They hung out under the shade of an umbrella, naked for a while, drying off nicely, though Océano's bruises looked terrible in broad daylight. As people started crowding the beach, they threw on their clothes again. Océano gave up on his bandages, which were now dirty looking and covered in sand.

"I'll be okay," he said as they sauntered back up the hill.

They wandered from shop to shop, admiring the latest designer beach and club wear. Chenche grabbed Demetrio at one point and kissed his cheek.

"You are doing great," he said before idling up to look at knock-off sunglasses at a barrow cart.

Demetrio had no idea what these mysterious words meant, but Océano was on his phone now, having what looked like a tense conversation. Demetrio checked his cell phone, which had been turned on, but he was anxious. There was still no word from Jeanine. They all walked to her apartment, knocked on her door, and left a note. She didn't turn up to clean, so as Océano walked over to Can Alfredo for lunch with Stefan and Chenche, Demetrio cleaned the place himself.

He was disgruntled Océano was off having fun, then forced a reminder on himself. *We're not a couple. He doesn't want me. There are no strings attached.*

His cell phone rang and he grabbed it. A long-distance call. It was Stella, his cousin John's widow. Her voice sounded wonderful. She sounded cheery and mentioned she was going to Paris to take a cooking course.

"That's fantastic," he said enthusiastically. She rarely left England and had never accepted an invitation to visit him in Eivissa.

"I've been hearing about the fugitive in Ibiza," she said. "I can't believe that he had amnesia and now he's recovered his memory and he's some kind of crooked cop."

"He's nothing of the sort." Demetrio couldn't help being defensive. He couldn't tell Stella what he knew. He'd promised Océano.

"Don't be ridiculous," Stella said, her voice instantly stern. "My wonderful husband, a man who never harmed anyone, vanished, and we couldn't save him. He died alone—"

"Yes, I know." Demetrio felt wretched.

"And this . . . this *monster* who shot his own partner . . . how does he get to live? I hear he was in Barcelona and Madrid, spending money like water . . . money that wasn't his. He has a trail of devastated women behind him, but he survives. It's wrong. Just wrong! He should be dead, not John!"

He couldn't calm her down. He understood, and it was unusual outburst for such a kind woman. Stella still grieved John. She would probably never get over him.

"Oh, Demetrio, you always were a sucker for a handsome face and a line of bull," she said, hanging up on him.

Their conversation shocked him. He knew that Stella still pined for her husband. Of course she did. But her rage at Océano was simply irrational. Life was like that. Goddamned bloody random. Blaming Océano for surviving was wrongheaded.

He thought about calling her back but knew that no good could come of any discussion at the moment. He turned on the radio to listen to any news bulletins. Not a word about Océano or Jeanine. He was loading up the fridges with beer from the cellar when he heard someone shouting his name. He looked up from unpacking crates, surprised to see Charlie at the door.

"I heard the cops are still looking for Jeanine," he said when Demetrio let him into the club.

"Where did you hear that?"

"I've got a mate on the force. Listen, I know you're friendly with Océano or whatever the fuck his real name is, but just be careful, yeah?"

Demetrio felt a sense of indignity swelling within him, but didn't give voice to it. Charlie was absolutely right and he seemed to care.

"I will," he said, taken aback when the man stepped behind the bar and started pulling out bottles to refrigerate. "You don't have to do that."

"Don't be silly. You need help." Charlie leaned over the crate. "We need anything else from the basement?"

"Two more crates, and thanks for the help."

"What's going on here?"

Both men straightened. Océano was on the other side of the bar, leaning over and watching them, a look of fury on his face.

"Loading up the fridge," Demetrio said.

Charlie picked up the empties. "Just two crates from the basement?"

"Yes, thank you, Charlie." The bartender gave him a smile and took off. Demetrio returned his gaze to Océano, who stared at him, a muscle working in his cheek. For a guy who wasn't gay and didn't want him, he sure was acting like a jealous jackass.

"We finished lunch. They've gone home for a siesta. I thought maybe you might feel like it . . . you know . . ."

Océano's voice drifted off when Demetrio didn't respond.

"You had lunch, but I didn't. I need to eat; then I thought I'd take a drive around the island."

Océano's expression faltered. "Really? You want to do that?"

"Yes."

"Oh. No siesta?"

"No siesta."

Demetrio bit the inside of his cheek to stop himself from laughing. The guy looked so disappointed. Yeah, Océano was definitely about as gay as Christmas, and twice as merry.

"Want to come with me?" he asked.

"Well . . . er . . . sure."

They spent a fun afternoon driving around the northern part of the island, stopping to walk through the pine forest, which had become the focal point of local conservation. One section had been reserved to introduce olive trees into it, as a means of new revenue for the future. It sure smelled good, the mixture of olives and pine. "I had a small fantasy," he told Océano when they returned his car to its parking spot, a garage he rented from an elderly couple.

"Oh, what kind of small fantasy?"

"That you stayed right here in Eivissa, and we rent a house up in the mountains, and you are nice and safe and nobody needs to know you're here, and I keep going to work every day and we can just be together, and when you need to be in England to go on trial, I'd go with you."

"That is a nice fantasy." Océano's face took on a closed expression as they walked to the club. "I have some calls to make." He crossed the street, walking away from Demetrio. He didn't come back.

Later, after he'd closed up the club, Demetrio wandered across the street to Sugar, but the place was too packed. Silver confetti fell from the ceiling. He remembered now, as strobe lights flashed and scantily clad men in silver bikini pants danced on pedestals high on the walls, that the club was celebrating the wedding of some visiting gay-porn stars who had married in Madrid and were honeymooning in Eivissa.

He caught Stefan's eye. Stefan waved him over, handing him a glass of champagne.

"You've missed all the fun. We had a live sex show!"

Demetrio laughed. "And the police didn't close you down?"

Stefan was wide-eyed. "No! They came, but it was all over by then. We raised a thousand euros. Half for Allister's memorial, and the other half for the children's hospital. You know Chenche loves to give them money."

Demetrio knew it very well. At Christmas Stefan and Chenche had held a party at the hospital for all the children who were stuck in there for the holidays. He'd been dazzled by how kind and generous the couple was, and how much they genuinely enjoyed giving the children a day to remember.

"That's fantastic," Demetrio said. "You seen Océano?"

"The police took him away. I think they had questions. Maybe he'll come back. Demetrio, please. Be careful. The man who came into your bar last night . . . he's very dangerous. He's been all over the news. He's some kind of hitman."

"Oh my God, and he's got Jeanine."

Stefan checked his cell phone. "Let's hope not. He's got a trail of dead bodies behind him. Just protect yourself, okay?"

Demetrio nodded. He went home but found he couldn't sleep. He had a stack of books on his nightstand, the words swam on the pages of each one he tried. At first light he drifted to sleep, finally, but a sound awakened him. Sighing, he got out of bed, went into the bathroom to pee, and came back out.

"You know," a voice said from behind him, "you really do look better naked."

Demetrio's shock at another presence in his room was quickly replaced by his joy at hearing Océano's voice. He turned and hurled himself into the other man's arms.

Océano looked terrible.

"They interrogated me for hours," he said. "I fucking hate my life right now." He furrowed his brows. "Except for this very moment."

A car horn honked. "I have to go. I told them I was picking up my things. Demetrio, don't come out. I don't want to look at you when I leave you. I don't want them to guess what we feel for each other. Fuck . . . I don't want to walk away from you."

"Then don't. Take me with you."

Océano kissed him. It was such a passionate kiss it left them both shaking. "It's another beautiful fantasy. I hope one day I get to see your face again. Forget about me, D. I can only bring you pain."

"No. I love you."

"Fuck! Don't love me."

"Sorry, but I do."

"Forget me. I'm sorry. I'm not the one for you."

The car horn honked again, and Océano picked up the plastic bag from the hospital with his few meager possessions. And with that he was gone.

Demetrio sat on the bed for a long time, cursing himself for telling the man he loved him.

What made me do it? Why? What the fuck was I thinking?

CHAPTER SIX

Océano, real name John Delancey, returned to London under armed escort feeling numb. Nothing seemed to compute. He'd done everything the force had asked of him. Yes, he'd been caught in a double-cross, and he'd done the unthinkable—he'd returned from the job without his partner. It looked bad. Questions had been asked and more would still be asked, but one issue remained.

Who'd told the bad guys their real identity? Who was behind it? Who had framed him and killed Joshua?

He still had dreams of the gunshot that killed his partner and best friend. He fought the images but fought harder than hell to forget about Demetrio Reyes.

Why had he lied and told the man he was straight? He wasn't. But being gay had been his deadly secret. Only one man knew about his true sexuality.

Joshua.

He had urged John to fake being straight, both because he didn't want a gay partner and because he believed John would be safer on the squad if no one knew he was a woofter. He winced, thinking of the disparaging way Joshua would refer to gay men. He remembered how the bad guys had derided him, calling him queer. He'd been stunned because he was so careful to cover his tracks whilst being undercover. He had bedded women, even snorted a bit of coke and boozed it up with the lads at a strip club or two.

John closed his eyes, the smell of lemons and pine strong in his mind.

He'd never met anyone like Demetrio. Dear, loving Demetrio, whose big hurt eyes would forever haunt him. He'd lied to save the man, to protect him from the fantasy that could never be real. He wanted Demetrio to move on, to be safe.

And yet he yearned to be with him.

If only I could have forgotten a little longer. If only I could forget who I am forever.

The sad thing is, I can see myself living there with him. But I don't see us living in the old town square. I see us being high in the mountains in one of those old houses near the orchards.

Oh God. What if he meets someone else?

The two-and-a-half-hour flight was over too soon.

It's a fantasy, he told himself over and over again.

No, it's not. This was his mother's voice in his head. When he was a kid, before he lost her, before she walked out on him and his dad, she'd said to him, "Remember, Johnny. This world is a lonely, tough place. People do things out of greed and fear. Those things exist, but only love is real."

The media came out in full force for his arrival at Gatwick.

I wonder if Demetrio is watching me now? Maybe he's too busy setting up his bar, carefully arranging his cheeses. I never did pay him back for all the food I ate. I wonder how Luis is? Do his fingers still hurt?

Maybe I could call when I get some time. No, I can't. I broke Demetrio's heart.

He looked down at the ground as cameras flashed and reporters asked rude questions. He knew the handcuffs and the stern expressions on the faces of the cops accompanying him were a formality, but still, it humiliated him.

I miss Eivissa. I miss the man I was there. I miss him.

Things weren't as bad as he'd expected at Scotland Yard. He met with his bosses, the same ones who had devised this scheme in the first place. A few faces had changed, but what hadn't changed was the dreary excuse for spring weather visible from the windows of the conference room.

He remembered the killer cocktails he'd shared with Demetrio. The wonderful night at the Golden Buddha with the sun setting as they laughed and joked.

Then he remembered waking up to find Luis standing over him and the crazy plastic penis he wore around his neck, and almost laughed.

I never got to smell almond blossoms with Demetrio. I'll never see him laugh again.

His life was on the line here, and all he could think about was how he and Luis often fought over the last slice of *flaó*, a sweetened goat cheese flan Demetrio bought fresh every day.

He struggled to concentrate. He knew he still looked awful and there were gaps in his memory. They asked strange questions about side deals with Syrian terrorists he clearly knew nothing about. It began to look like Joshua had double-crossed him, duped them all, leaving the woofter holding an empty bag.

Her Majesty's coffers had been bled dry during their sting operation. They had both taken money out of a certain bank account to buy drugs and weapons, but in his furtive calls and e-mails to his immediate bosses, John had accounted for everything he spent.

In the final weeks of the operation, when he and Joshua met the heads of the big drug operation, all communication had ceased. Money kept vanishing from the account.

"It wasn't me," John insisted. "The one meal I took the main guy to, what was his name? Christian something. Man, I'm sorry. My memory comes back in snatches. Boulerman. That's what it was. I took him to dinner in Madrid and used the credit card you gave me."

Questions and more questions.

"We'll be in touch," the chief superintendent told him. "As of now you're on unpaid leave until we complete our investigation."

Unpaid leave? "But I have no money," he said. "I gave up my flat when I went undercover. I have no place to go."

"You've got your dad," one of the men at the table said, his sneer evident.

My dad. Oh God. Are things as bad as that?

They did show some mercy. He'd had a bank account that had accrued money in his absence. His paycheck had gone into it and one of the force's accountants had maintained it for him. He hadn't been allowed to touch it during his under-cover operation, but now the accountant accompanied him to the branch of the Bank of England closest to the Yard, and helped procure him a Visa debit card. He was given a tempo-rary card and activated the pin.

"Where do we send the new card to?" the personal banker asked John. He could practically hear the accountant snorting as he recited his father's address on St. David Road in the Isle of Dogs.

What was it about his father that made them all behave like idiots? Yes, he'd been a mediocre detective who'd retired when his drinking became excessive. But he was the one who tipped them off on many illegal activities in the once-rough and violent wharfside neighborhood.

The Isle of Dogs, or The Island as locals called it, had be-come *the* place to live. John Delancey, Sr. had invested his money and had become a hot property developer. The cop-pers he'd left behind resented his freedom, probably. And his income.

"Use this cell phone," the accountant said. "Let us know where you land."

And with that he turned on his heel, leaving John to his own devices. He took some money out of the ready teller, bought a pass for the tube, and went to his old home in Ken-sington. The apartment on the Vicarage Gate looked the same as ever, but somebody else was enjoying it now. He stood on the corner, looking up at the brownstone building, wondering what he'd expected. A 'to let' sign awaiting his return?

He suddenly remembered that, once upon a time, he'd actually walked down to the vicarage itself and sat down for a cup of tea with the vicar.

"I want to know the meaning of life," he'd told the man, who really had no answer.

He looked up at the sky, pondering his next move. He'd have to go home to the old bastard who hated him. John Delancey, Sr. was charming and full of toothy smiles to everyone he met, except his son. John had always seemed to irritate him. Perhaps because he'd been forced to raise him singlehandedly. He'd been a harsh father until John turned twenty-one, when he treated him like an old friend.

There was nothing for it but to head to The Island. Not that he wanted to. The only island he really wanted was the one two and a half hours away.

He checked the time on his new cell phone.

What is Demetrio doing now? Is he walking in his beloved forest? Is he cleaning the bar? Is he sleeping?

He ached and itched to call the man, but didn't.

John Delancey, Jr. took the tube to the other island and was surprised to find the former trash heap looking more gorgeous than ever.

As he arrived at street level, he turned in circles, staring at all the mirrored windows. He thought about the disco ball at Club Sugar and thought he might never be happy again.

Demetrio fell asleep for about ten minutes. The radio sounded and he listened to the ten o'clock morning news bulletin. "Police extradited Detective John Delancey back to London this morning. Delancey, who washed up on the shores of Eivissa, is wanted in connection with the shooting death of his partner, Joshua Riley, in a drug deal gone sour."

Demetrio listened to it. John Delancey. Océano was really

John. How weird he shared the same name as his cousin. One was lost, one was found. Both were gone. Move on.

But I can't.

As the days wore on, it seemed to Demetrio they only became more hellish. He read the newspapers, relying on the internet versions of British newspapers for more detailed information. John Delancey was portrayed as either a good cop gone bad or a good cop being railroaded, depending on which source was being quoted. The bloody *Daily Mail* was following him and had taken photos of him looking particularly gaunt and hollow-eyed when he'd gone shopping for coffee and a box of Ready Brek at Tesco on the Canary Wharf one morning. The online rag made John sound like a lonely loser with his apparent breakfast for one. They also quoted women from three different continents describing his heavy partying and endless lies.

When the blond man who'd been in Club Dino, now identified as Christian Boulerman, a British industrialist turned wannabe arms dealer, was arrested in Barcelona, Demetrio felt relief, especially when Jeanine was discovered in bed with him, unharmed. She was all over CNN but returned to Ibiza and her beloved cats. Demetrio let her talk on the night she came back. "I should have gone out with my massage client, but he seemed boring," she told him. "Boring seems so appealing to me now." Tears fell from her eyes. "I can read other people but I'm hopeless when it comes to me." She seemed dazed when she described her romance with Boulerman as "passionate, intense, and dangerous."

Some idiot filmmaker showed up on Eivissa, anxious to secure the film rights to her story, and soon departed when Jeanine refused to speak to him. A few days later, Boulerman issued a public denial via his attorney that anything had ever transpired between him and Jeanine.

"I'm very loyal to my wife. I'd never cheat on her,"

Boulerman said. "I have no idea how she got into my bed." Within hours, three other women came forward claiming to be former mistresses. He insisted he had no idea how he managed to appear naked in dozens of photos with them.

"What a doucheweed," Jeanine announced as she and Demetrio watched the report on Chenche's new, gigantic flat-screen TV one night over dinner at the new terrace house Chenche and Stefan had just bought. It was the only funny moment in an otherwise ongoing drama for Demetrio. One week turned into two, and Jeanine returned to Club Dino to work. The gay contingent seemed to love her more because Boulerman had publicly dissed her. She in turn seemed to adore their sympathy.

And suddenly, Eivissa's homeless cat population had a mighty network of desperate adopters.

"I should get loved and dumped more," she joked, but she'd finally accepted a date with the massage guy, and Demetrio hoped she'd settle for normal.

Demetrio meanwhile struggled to get through each day until one night, as he was closing the bar, his cell phone rang. His unknown caller turned out to be Océano.

"Are you closing?" Océano asked.

"Oh God." Demetrio almost dropped the phone. "I fucking miss you."

"Oh God," Océano moaned. "I can't believe I'm calling you."

They were silent for a moment. Demetrio worried about saying the wrong thing and pissing Océano off.

"Have you read the papers? You following what's going on?"

"Yes, and I don't believe a word of it. Is there really going to be a trial?"

"So they say. Why are you so sure I'm innocent?"

"I just know it."

"So you believe me?"

"Yes. Of course I do."

"I don't know whether you're the most amazing person I ever met or the stupidest. There are people I've known for years who've turned their backs on me."

"I'm sorry."

"Yeah. Me, too."

A pause.

"Demetrio, you seeing anybody?"

"No. I'm no slut. I'm still waiting for you to come back. We all miss you."

"Shit." Océano blew out a sigh. "I gotta go, sweetheart. I'm staying with my old man and he's in a bad mood. I can already tell." His voice dropped. "Be good."

He ended the call. Demetrio wanted to scream at the sky, at Océano, and everything in between. He tried to lose the wishbone in his back. He had to get over this man and move on. Over the next few nights, he tried dating but felt inexplicably like he was cheating on Océano.

As the days wore on, he hoped and prayed for another call. He heard on the news that John Delancey was getting married. Ironically the announcement came the same day Allister's memorial bench and pine tree were ready to be implemented at a bluff overlooking the sea.

Most of the club and café owners came to the small ceremony. They planted the tree, lit some candles, and cemented the bench into the ground. For days Demetrio returned to the bench to watch the ocean and to think about the man that the sea had brought him. On the fourth day, he was surprised when Chenche showed up to sit beside him.

"You shouldn't be sad," Chenche said.

"I miss him. I wish I didn't."

"Yes. I know." Chenche put his arm around him.

"He's getting married."

Chenche kissed his cheek. "No, he's not. He loves you. I saw how he looked at you. You must have faith. You are a child of Eivissa. You must believe in love. You must believe in the sea. This is your church, right here. Be patient. The sea will bring him back."

He was shocked that Chenche of all people would give him a speech like this. He could imagine it from Stefan, but not from Chenche.

"Thank you," he said, humbled by the man's friendship.

"You know, I was straight once. I panicked when I discovered I like cock. It's hard to realize you love a man. I did stupid things. *¡Estúpido!* But you'll see. Océano, he likes cock, too. A lot." His grin made Demetrio laugh.

That night he received a strange call: 'Unknown caller,' and not a word was spoken. There was a strange spacey sound in the background. He wanted to think it was Océano. He liked to think they were swirling in the ocean together, arm in arm, lovers in love. The line went dead.

"You all right, son?"

John almost jumped ten feet into the air.

"Yeah, Dad. I'm okay."

The old man set a beer on the coffee table and eased himself onto the sofa. He always kept his leather jacket on, like he might just walk out the door. John hadn't even heard him enter the apartment. John Sr. was a solid two-beer-a-day guy now and happily dating a woman John Jr. liked, but it didn't look like it was going anywhere.

"You're the unhappiest man I've ever met," his father suddenly said.

"That's the pot calling the kettle black." John instantly regretted the words. The littlest thing could set his father off, drunk or sober.

The old man lifted his shoulders. "I am exactly what it says on the tin." He leaned forward, grabbed the beer, and pointed the neck toward his son. "You, on the other hand, you're a mystery man, all right. You look like you should be happy. You got yourself a great girl, but I can tell you don't love her. You got off all charges. And okay, I know they retired you from active duty, but you resigned and got a full pension and wages for two years. The world is yours. Do what you want with it."

John said nothing. It wasn't as easy as that. He had to do something, and he knew it. But nothing made him happy. He was only happy when he was sleeping.

"Do something, ya daft cunt. Don't end up a lonely old bastard like me."

John stared at his father, who put the beer to his lips and drained the bottle dry.

After the silent phone call, Demetrio went out that night, looking for a sign to either give up hope or to hang on. The first song he heard over at Sugar was a remix of the song 'Return to Innocence,' with its recurring refrain of 'hold on, hold on, hold on.'

Emboldened, he kept looking for signs. He spent his time with Stefan and Chenche. He tried to be positive, even when the newspapers stopped reporting on the strange case of John Delancey. Even the gossip on Eivissa stopped. A new current came with the changes of the tide. There were new things to talk about. New songs. New fashions. New people.

Demetrio dated a ton of guys but never let anyone get close enough for even a goodnight kiss. His heart kept pounding at his head, 'hold on, hold on, hold on.'

One morning he awoke before the alarm rang. He had the urge to peruse the online reports and was intrigued to learn all charges against John Delancey had been dropped. He was too high profile to be a further asset in his career as an undercover officer, and he'd resigned from the force.

Was he forced to resign?

His impending wedding plans were dropped, his fiancée griping to reporters that he was a cold fish.

Demetrio laughed when he read that. Cold fish? Not the John Delancey he knew. He lay back in bed, his iPad on his lap, wondering what John Delancey and/or Océano would do next. His clock radio went off, and the song playing was an old Wilson Phillips song, 'Hold On.'

He found himself smiling. If he ever dared tell anyone how these words kept coming to him, how he found strength and conviction in holding on, people would think he was crazy. He left the house, picking some flowers along the way, and went to visit Allister's bench. He left the flowers tied to the bench, next to a red balloon left over from a bunch of them Chenche had left there a few days before.

Demetrio wandered the streets, thinking about things. He had an unrealistic yet relentless sense of anticipation. He found himself feeling euphoric as the day wore on.

"You seem really happy," Jeanine said to him as they cleaned the club.

He shrugged. "Not really." But really, he was. Yes. He was happy. All he heard in his mind was 'hold on.' He was bursting with the feeling something was about to happen. She tried to question him, but he went to the basement to bring up crates. He felt better than he had in days. He just wanted to live with this feeling of lightness, even if it evaporated like water in the hot sun.

Back upstairs, his cell phone rang. A text message. *Meet me at the old church on the mountain. I am here. I miss you.*

Fuck! It had to be Océano ... didn't it? Christ, what if it was Chenche, or worse, some guy he'd dated? No. It had to be Océano. But why the church? Why not just walk in here and lay claim to Demetrio?

"I gotta go," he said to Jeanine, leaving the crate on the floor.

"Whatever," she said, pushing the broom around, a sour look on her face.

He retrieved his car and drove up the mountain. He parked, disheartened not to see another car in the spaces reserved for hikers. He hesitated for a moment. He hadn't told anyone where he was. He put a quick call in to Stefan and left a voice message telling him he was on a hike.

"See you soon," he said. He ended the call and began walking.

By the time he got to the church an hour later he'd worked up a good sweat Not a soul was there. Inside it was empty. He left some money in the collection box. Outside he tried to swallow his disappointment.

Where to now?

He wandered aimlessly through the grounds as he checked the text message. It had, of course, come from an unknown caller.

"You know," a voice said from behind him, "I think you might have the finest ass on Eivissa."

Demetrio stuttered to a stop. His heart pounded in his constricted chest. He didn't think he was hearing things. It had to be Océano. Just because his tender heart wanted it to be real, he didn't think he was hallucinating. God couldn't be that cruel.

He could have said a million things in that moment, but his heart ached with the pain of the last two months. Better to keep things light.

"You only *think* it's the finest ass?"

"No, I'm pretty certain."

A beat.

"Turn around, Demetrio."

Demetrio turned, trying to keep his gaze down, urging himself not to cry.

"I'm sorry I stayed away, sweetheart. I've really missed you. You are the only one who loved and believed in me."

Love. My God . . . he said the word.

"It's strange how you can meet someone and just have instincts about them. I knew I wanted to be with you even when I couldn't understand it. I'd never explored my feelings for a man. I think . . . I mean, I *really* think I might have had feelings for Joshua, but I'll never know. We let the chance slip by, and now he's gone. But I'll be damned if I'm gonna let another wonderful man get away from me. I don't want any more missed chances. Not with you, Demetrio. Each and every day I've panicked, wondering if some idiot guy's gonna walk into your bar and sweep you off your feet."

Demetrio said nothing. Tears kept falling from his eyes. He kept seeing his cousin John in his mind's eye. John walking in circles, feeling alone.

"I'm here," Océano finally said, and covered the distance between them, taking him into his arms. "I'm sorry I stayed away so long. I'm sorry for every moment of pain I've given you."

Their mouths collided, Demetrio not sure it was even real as they kissed with such savage passion he was having trouble breathing.

Océano pushed him to the ground. "If you'll let me, I want to be with you. I want what you told me we have. I want a life with you."

Demetrio felt the man moving above him, tears falling from Océano's eyes and onto Demetrio's face.

"You wanted me to fuck you in the grass and I never got the chance. I knew if I came to the club, I'd be in danger of fucking you right there, taking you in front of everybody." He glued his mouth to Demetrio's, preventing any response.

They fumbled at each other's clothing, mouths and fingers and tongues in hot pursuit. He felt Océano's hot cock poking at him, Demetrio opening his legs as Océano prepared to fuck him.

"Tell me you want it, too," Océano. "If you don't . . . fuck, then I want to die."

"I want it," Demetrio said as Océano entered him. Their mingled cries rang out as the bells of the old church pealed. That was the sound of Eivissa — music, love, and old church bells.

"I love you," Océano shouted above the sound of the bells as he fucked Demetrio, reaching between their bodies to hold Demetrio's cock.

Demetrio would have responded except that Océano's tongue was in his mouth, his breath squashed out of him. He grappled for the man's ass as Océano moved into him with quickening strokes. He smelled grass and sex as the bells stopped ringing, and all that was left was love.

Hold on, his heart said. *Just hold on.*

ABOUT THE AUTHOR

A.J. Llewellyn is the author of over 300 M/M romance novels. She was born in Australia, and lives in Los Angeles. An early obsession with Robinson Crusoe led to a lifelong love affair with islands, particularly Hawaii and Easter Island.

Being marooned once on Wedding Cake Island in Australia cured her of a passion for fishing, but led to a plotline for a novel. A.J.'s friends live in fear because even the smallest details of their lives usually wind up in her stories. A.J. has a desire to paint, draw, juggle, work for the FBI, walk a tightrope with an elephant, be a chess champion, a steeplejack, master chef, and a world-class surfer. She can't do any of these things so she writes about them instead.

A.J. started life as a journalist and boxing columnist, and still enjoys interrogating, er, interviewing people to find out what makes them tick.

How to find/friend me:

email: ajllewellyn@gmail.com
website: www.ajllewellyn.com
www.facebook.com/aj.llewellyn
www.twitter.com/ajllewellyn
Newsletter sign-up: ajllewellynnewsletter@gmail.com—
each month I give away a free ebook!
I'm an app! Download my FREE A.J. Llewellyn App for Android here: http://tinyurl.com/lkbc4wm

www.ingramcontent.com/pod-product-compliance
Lightning Source LLC
Chambersburg PA
CBHW060646130626
46555CB00002B/979